P9-DEQ-365

MOBY DICK

HERMAN MELVILLE

CONDENSED AND ADAPTED BY
W.T. ROBINSON

ILLUSTRATED BY
JERRY DILLINGHAM

Dalmatian 🐾 Press™

The Dalmatian Press Children's Classics Collection
has been adapted and illustrated with care and thought,
to introduce you to a world of famous authors, characters, ideas,
and great stories that have been loved for generations.

Editor — Kathryn Knight
Creative Director — Gina Rhodes
And the entire classics project team of Dalmatian Press

ALL ART AND EDITORIAL MATERIAL OWNED BY DALMATIAN PRESS, LLC

ISBN: 1-57759-539-4 mass
1-57759-547-5 base

First Published in the United States in 2001 by Dalmatian Press, LLC, USA

Copyright©2001 Dalmatian Press, LLC

Printed and bound in the U.S.A.

The DALMATIAN PRESS name and spotted spine logo are
trademarks of Dalmatian Press, LLC, Franklin, Tennessee 37067.

All rights reserved. Written permission must be secured from
the publisher to use or reproduce any part of this book,
except for brief quotations in critical reviews or publicity.

11384

02 03 04 LBM 10 9 8 7 6 5 4

A note to the reader—

A classic story rests in your hands. The characters are famous. The tale is timeless.

Although this is not the original version (which you really *must* read when you're ready for every detail), this Dalmatian Press Children's Classic has been shortened and adapted especially for you. We kept the well-known phrases for you. We kept the author's style. And we kept the important imagery and heart of the tale.

Literature is terrific fun! It encourages you to think. It helps you dream. It is full of heroes and villains, suspense and humor, adventure and wonder, and new ideas. It introduces you to writers who reach out across time to say: "Do you want to hear a story I wrote?"

Curl up and enjoy.

DALMATIAN PRESS
ILLUSTRATED CLASSICS

ALICE'S ADVENTURES IN WONDERLAND

ANNE OF GREEN GABLES

BLACK BEAUTY

THE CALL OF THE WILD

THE STORY OF
DOCTOR DOLITTLE

THE STRANGE CASE OF
DR. JEKYLL AND MR. HYDE

HEIDI

THE ADVENTURES OF
HUCKLEBERRY FINN

A LITTLE PRINCESS

LITTLE WOMEN

MOBY DICK

OLIVER TWIST

PETER PAN

THE SECRET GARDEN

THE TIME MACHINE

THE ADVENTURES OF
TOM SAWYER

TREASURE ISLAND

THE WONDERFUL WIZARD OF OZ

CONTENTS

ISHMAEL — that's me, the teller of this tale, a young man who goes to sea on a whaling ship

PETER COFFIN — the innkeeper of *The Spouter Inn*

QUEEQUEG — a tattooed South Sea native, an expert harpooner, my good friend

PELEG AND CAPTAIN BILDAD — the owners of our ship, the *Pequod*

CAPTAIN AHAB — a dark sea captain with one cry— "Have ye seen the White Whale?"

STARBUCK — chief mate on the *Pequod*, a good man with a wise heart

STUBB — second mate, a cheery sailor who smokes a pipe

FLASK — third mate, a short, tough sailor

TASHTEGO — a long, lean American Indian, Stubb's harpooner

DAGGOO — a giant African, Flask's harpooner

FEDALLAH — a mysterious man with a small band of nameless crewmen, Ahab's harpooner and advisor

Ships we meet on our long sail at sea:
  JEROBOAM
  SAMUEL ENDERBY
  BACHELOR
  RACHEL
  DELIGHT

MOBY DICK

CHAPTER ONE

A New Freedom

Call me Ishmael. A few years ago, with no money in my wallet and nothing interesting to do on shore, I thought I would sail around a little on the watery part of the world. There is something magic about being on the water and free of the land. I had been to sea many times before, but never to hunt whales. I don't know why, but this just seemed what I had to do this time. I would find a whaling ship and see if I could join the crew. The thrill of hunting the huge monster of the ocean and sailing the distant seas began to fill my mind. This was going to be exciting!

So, on a cold December morning, I stuffed a

shirt or two into an old suitcase and left my home for New Bedford, Massachusetts. From there I could take a ferry to Nantucket where I would get on a whaling ship.

I arrived in New Bedford on a cold, wet night. I could smell the ocean's salty air as I walked the New Bedford streets in search of a bed for the night. As I neared the waterfront, I saw a sign swinging in the wind that read *The Spouter Inn* – Peter Coffin. I liked the name of the place since I would be looking for whale spouts at sea. The owner's last name gave me a little shiver up my spine, but I would worry about that later. I went inside.

On one wall hung a painting of a huge whale about to attack a sinking ship. On another wall I saw a collection of old, rusted whaling spears, called harpoons, which are used to kill the giant fish. There were sailors sitting around carving things from the bones and teeth of whales.

Mr. Coffin told me he had no empty beds. "But wait," he said, "you can share a bed with a harpooner. If you are goin' whalin' you best get used to that sort of thing." I told him I never liked to sleep two to a bed. But I was too cold and

hungry to argue. I said I would give it a try.

At last, a good hot supper of meat, potatoes, and dumplings was served. "When will I meet this harpooner?" I asked the landlord. "What time does he go to bed?"

"Oh, you won't be seein' him for a long time yet, lad," Coffin said with a grin. "He's somewhere in town sellin' those shrunken heads he picks up in the South Sea islands."

Shrunken heads? I thought. Now I was too afraid to go to bed and too tired to stay awake. Finally, the landlord calmed me down a little and showed me to my room. Placing a candle on an old sea chest next to the bed, he wished me sweet dreams and left.

All I could think about was this harpooner and what sort of a night it was going to be. Gathering enough courage to get into bed, I put myself in God's care for the night. Whether that mattress was stuffed with corn cobs or broken dishes, I don't know, but I rolled and tossed a lot and could not sleep for a long time. I had finally slipped off into a light doze when I heard some heavy footsteps in the hall. A ray of light came into the room from under the door.

I lay perfectly still, waiting to see what would happen. Holding a light in one hand and a terrible shrunken head in the other, the stranger entered the room. Good heavens! What a sight! His face was a dark purplish yellow color, and there were tattoos all over his face and body. His hair was tied up in a knot on top of his head. After he placed his candle on the floor, he pulled something out of a big bag in the corner of the room. It looked like a tomahawk! I was scared, but I tried to lay still and remember that a man who is ugly on the outside can still be good on the inside. Just as I had begun to calm down a little, this huge, dark savage took a wooden black doll from within his coat. Then he lit a small fire from some wood chips and began praying a strange prayer. Finally, he blew out his candle and jumped into bed. I screamed out in fear.

"Who-ee debel you?" the dark stranger asked. "Speakee to me! You no speakee—I killee!"

"Save me! Save me, landlord!" I shouted. "Please help me!"

I heard some footsteps in the hall. When the landlord came into the room, I leaped from my bed and ran up to him.

"Don't be afraid," he said, grinning at me. "Queequeg here wouldn't harm a hair on your head."

The landlord spoke to Queequeg, telling him we were going to "sleepee" together, and everything would be fine. And he was right. Queequeg climbed quietly into bed. He no longer seemed so strange. Maybe he had been as afraid of me as I of him. He was peaceful and calm now as he drifted off to sleep. I rolled over and never slept better in my life.

The sun was just coming up when I awoke the next morning. Queequeg was snoring loudly. I looked at the colorful tattoos that covered his body. What an odd sight the first thing in the morning! I shook him gently, for I could not get out of bed until he awoke and moved—no luck. "Queequeg!"—more snores. Here I was, trapped next to a savage with a tomahawk at his side! "Queequeg, Queequeg, wake up!"

At last, with some grunts and groans, he got up, put on a tall hat and boots, and then began to wash and shave. But where was his razor? That was soon answered when he picked up his harpoon. Moving to a bit of mirror against the wall, he began to scrape (or should I say *harpoon*?) his cheeks. How sharp that harpoon must be!

After his shaving and bathing were complete, Queequeg finished dressing. Holding his harpoon before him as though he were leading a band, he proudly marched out of the room.

I quickly dressed and went downstairs to get some breakfast. Seated at the table were people such as I had never seen. There were whaling sailors of all kinds. I could see the effects of sun and salt-sea air on their tanned, cracked faces. They were a shaggy lot. There were chief mates, second mates, third mates, sea carpenters, barrel makers, blacksmiths, harpooners, cooks, and common deckhands. I joined the group just as a loud "Grub ho!" from the landlord told me that breakfast was on its way.

Queequeg sat at the head of the table, cool as an icicle. His manners were a bit strange, however. He had brought his harpoon to breakfast and began using it to reach across the length of the table to spear the beefsteaks. He ate none of the hot rolls, nor did he drink the hot coffee. He ate only the rarest of the steak. When he had enough, he sat back to relax and smoke his tomahawk, which to my surprise turned out to be his pipe.

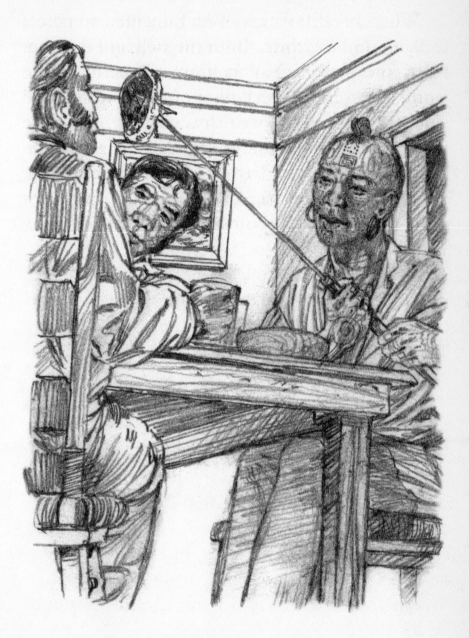

When breakfast was over, I decided to take a walk around the town. Both the rich and the poor filled the streets. Sailors from all parts of the world, dressed in every type of clothing, walked side by side with wealthy visitors from the nearby states of Vermont and New Hampshire. It was a Sunday, and I heard a preacher telling about Jonah and the Whale. That was not what I wanted to hear just before I went on my whale hunt!

CHAPTER TWO

A New Friend

When I returned to *The Spouter Inn*, I found Queequeg alone, quietly humming a tune and whittling the face of the wooden doll he called Yojo. I watched him for a while. There was a kindness in his eyes which must have come from inside his soul. He had a proud look. I thought that he must be a man of honesty and courage.

We talked a little, and I offered to help him understand a book he had taken off the shelf. He seemed thankful for my kindness and offered me a smoke. As we passed the pipe back and forth in the warmth of the small fire burning in our room, a change took place in our hearts. When our

smoke was finished, Queequeg pressed his forehead to mine and told me that we were now to be lifetime friends. He even said he would die for me if ever he had to.

The following morning it was time to find a ferry to Nantucket. I paid the bill for the stay at the inn and borrowed a wheelbarrow into which we loaded our things. The landlord was surprised to see the new friendship between Queequeg and me as he watched us heading off together for the dock.

We paid for our trip on the *Moss*, a small ship headed for Nantucket, and loaded our things on board. The breeze filled the small ship's sails. The salt air licked against my face. My thoughts turned to the sea. I took one last look at the land behind us.

CHAPTER THREE

The *Pequod*

It was nearly dark when we reached Nantucket. What a place it was—a small wind-blown island with no trees and very few plants. The Indians discovered the island many years ago. Then came the white men who first sailed from its shore in search of fish. Now, men sailed to all corners of the world from this tiny seaport. Mr. Coffin had told us that his cousin, Hosea Hussey, owned an inn called *The Try Pots*. After wandering around and getting lost several times, we finally found the place. Mr. Hussey's wife served us some delicious soup of clams and codfish. I was glad to see that Queequeg didn't

try to harpoon the small pieces of fish in the soup as he had speared the steaks earlier in the day. After supper, we went upstairs to bed. Tomorrow we would find a ship and prepare to go on a great adventure.

I woke early, and, while Queequeg was still having his morning prayers with Yojo, I found my way down to the docks. There were several whaling ships. One caught my eye. It was named *Pequod*. Although its decks were old and battered, the three tall poles, called masts, which held the sails, stood tall and straight. Spying a small tent near the docked ship, I peeked inside.

"Are you the captain of the *Pequod*?" I asked the man seated in the tent.

"I am an owner of the ship ye name," the old sailor answered in a rough voice. "Who wants to know?"

"My name is Ishmael. I and a friend of mine want to sign up to go hunting whales on your ship."

"Well, my name is Peleg, and what do ye know about whaling, young lad?" the owner asked.

"I don't know much," I confessed. "But I've worked on other kinds of ships, and I want to learn. Please give me a try."

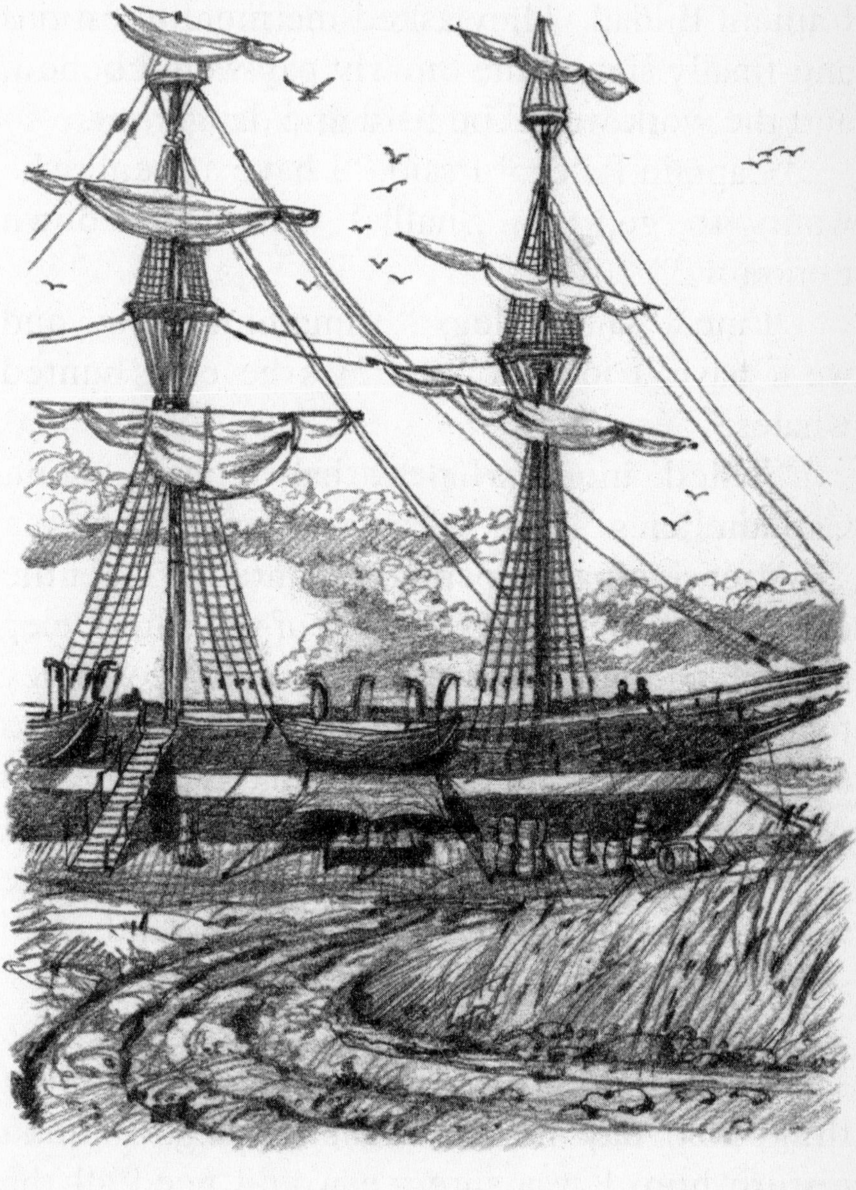

Peleg took me to the other owner of the ship, Captain Bildad. They asked me more questions and finally signed me on. My pay would be low, and the work would be hard and dangerous.

"Captain Peleg," I said, "I have a friend who wants to go, too. Shall I bring him down tomorrow?"

"Fine," said Peleg. "Bring him along, and we'll have a look at him. Has he ever hunted whales?"

"Killed more whales than I can count, Captain Peleg."

After signing the papers, I wanted to meet the man who would sail as captain of the ship. Peleg and Bildad told me I would meet him later. They told me that he could be a good man and a terrible one at the same time. His name was Ahab, and he had lost a leg fighting a whale. As I walked away, I thought about this strange Captain Ahab. A man with a good side and a bad side could be hard to work for.

When I arrived back at the inn that evening, Mrs. Hussey told me that Queequeg had spent the whole day in the room praying. I didn't disturb him. I was sure we would need all the

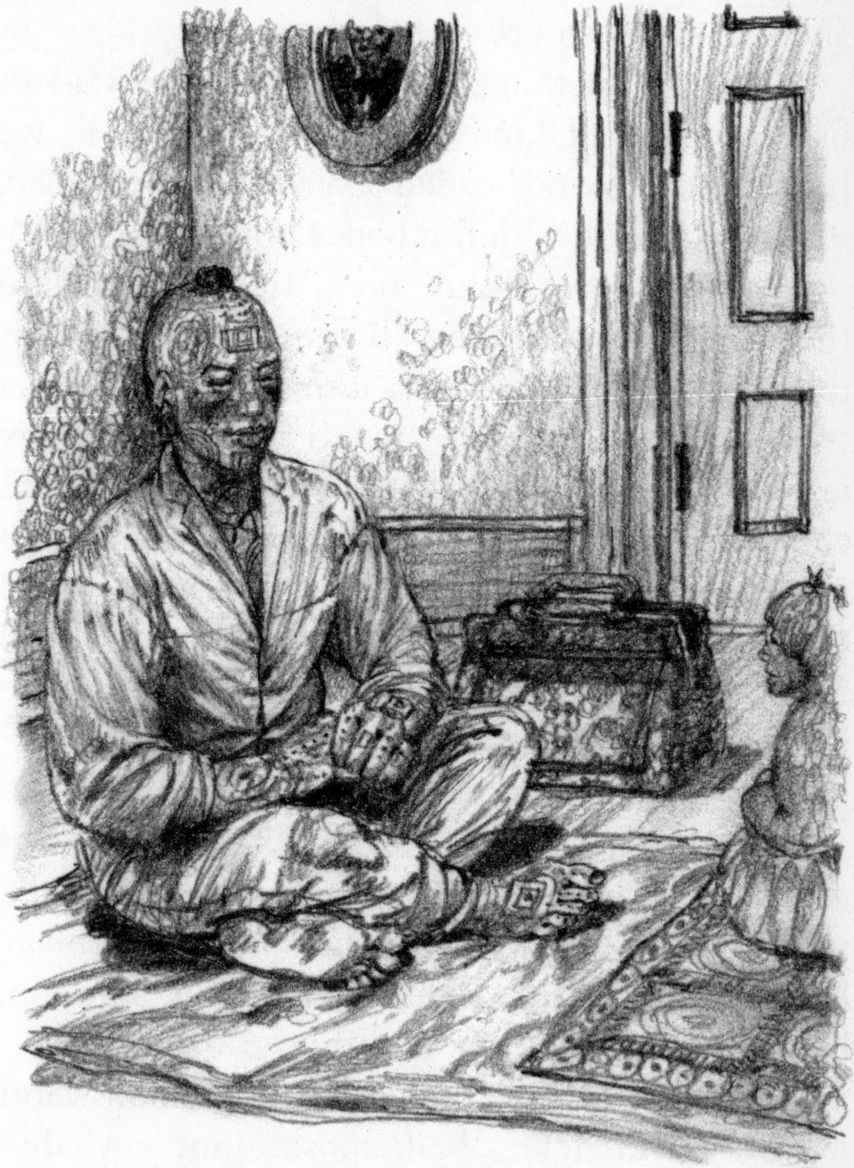

prayers we could get. I quietly crawled into bed and was soon asleep.

The next morning, we ate a huge breakfast of fish soups of all kinds. When we were full, we packed our bags and headed out to get on the *Pequod*, picking our teeth with fish bones along the way.

As we were walking along the dock toward the ship, Captain Peleg shouted at us from his tent saying I had not told him my friend was a wild-looking savage. I argued strongly for my tattooed friend. I said that we were all God's children and that they would find Queequeg a man they could trust. They still made fun of Queequeg, even his name.

"Quohog, Hedgehog, or whatever your name is, did ye ever stand at the head of a whaleboat? Did ye ever spear a fish?" cried Peleg.

Without saying a word—but with a wild gleam in his eye—Queequeg jumped over the ship's rails and into one of the small whaleboats hanging on the side. Then, raising his harpoon, he cried out something like this:

"Cap'ain, you see him small drop oil on water far away over dere? Well, sposee him a whale's eye den!" And taking sharp aim at it, he threw

the harpoon right past Bildad's head and hit the shining oil spot square in the center.

"Now," said Queequeg, quietly pulling in the line of the harpoon, "sposee him tar spot whalee eye. Well, dat whale dead!"

When they saw Queequeg's skill, the owners said he could join the crew. I was proud of my friend who, though he could not write, made his mark on the papers we were asked to sign. I noticed that it was the same mark as one of the tattoos on his arm. It had been a good morning. Things were looking bright.

A day or two passed, and there was a lot going on aboard the *Pequod* as it was loaded for the three-year trip. New sails were brought on board and old sails were being mended. Coils of rope, harpoons, food, water, empty barrels to store the whale oil, and every other thing you could imagine were stored below the ship's decks. But we had still not seen that strange Ahab.

With no captain to direct things, I was glad to hear one of the sailors say that our chief mate was bustling around. "Halloa! Starbuck's on the move," said the sailor. "He's a lively chief, he is, a good man and a religious one."

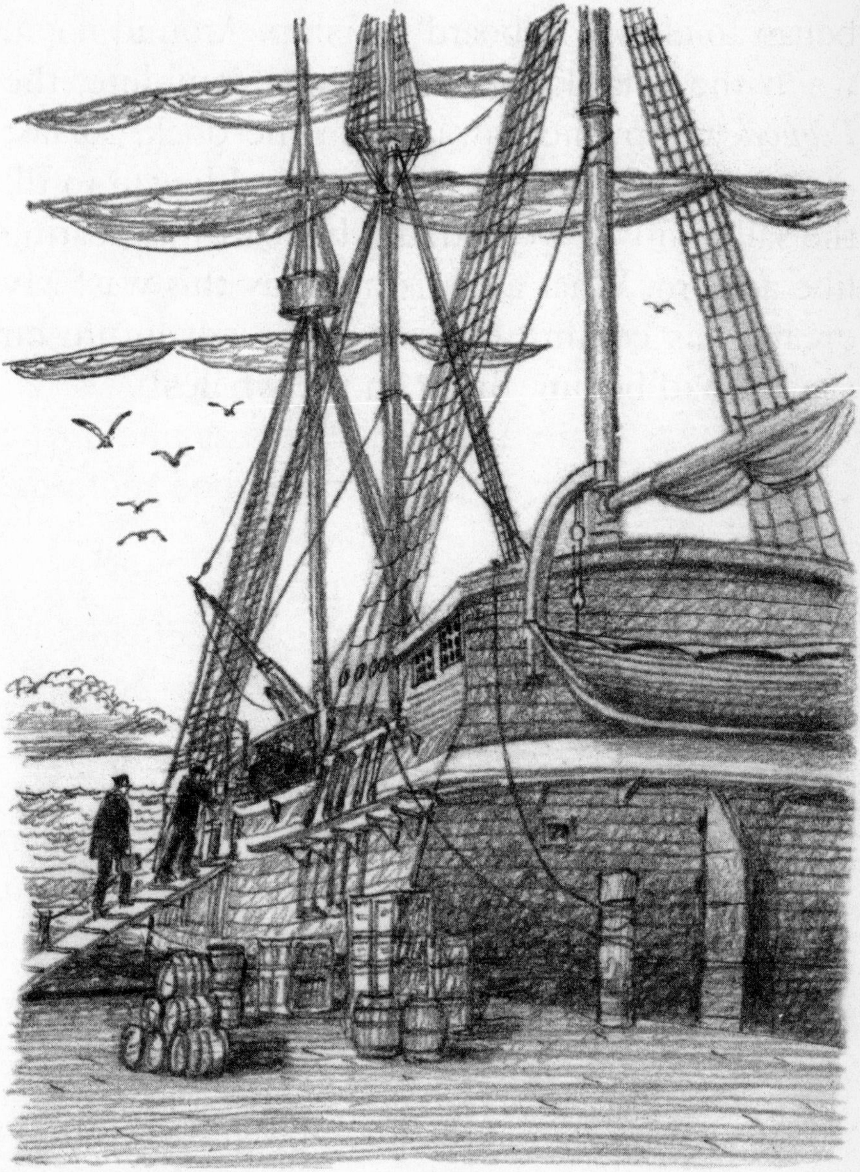

By now the sun was high in the sky. The crew began to climb on board the ship. Around noon, when the final list of duties was complete, the *Pequod* was pushed away from the dock. At last the anchor was pulled up, the wind began to fill the sails, and off we glided. My heart was beating like a drum. What a Christmas day this was! My dream was coming true. My new adventure on the sea had begun. Bring on the whales!

CHAPTER FOUR

Merry Christmas

It was a cold Christmas. As the day turned into night, we found ourselves upon a wintry ocean. A freezing spray wrapped us in ice. Like the white ivory tusks of some huge elephant, giant, curving icicles hung from the ship's rails.

Once we had reached a distance from shore, the two owners' work was done. A smaller boat, which had followed us out from Nantucket, pulled alongside to take Bildad and Peleg back to shore. The old sailors said their good-byes and wished us a safe journey.

"God bless ye, and keep ye, men," said Bildad. "I hope ye have fine weather. Don't

forget thy prayers. Be careful in the hunt, mates. Watch that leak in the molasses jug…" On and on he went, until Peleg finally told him it was past time to go. I could see that these old sailors missed going to sea and were putting off returning to land as long as they could. As they climbed into the boat headed back to shore, there were tears in the eyes of the tough whale hunters.

The smaller boat slowly disappeared from sight. A screaming bird flew over us. We gave three cheers and slid into the lonely Atlantic seas.

CHAPTER FIVE

Shipmates

Several days passed with not a sign of Captain Ahab. I did, however, meet the others of our crew. The chief mate of the *Pequod* was Starbuck, a native of Nantucket and a good person. He was a tall, slender man, but hard as nails. The rest of the men looked up to him because he was calm and steady. He was only thirty, but he seemed older. Perhaps the deaths of his father and brother during past whaling trips made him that way. He had great courage, but he was also very careful. He knew the dangers of hunting giant whales.

Stubb, the second mate, was from Cape Cod,

Massachusetts. He was happy and carefree and I was told he could be heard humming a tune right in the middle of a battle with a whale. Stubb had a pipe in his mouth all of the time. He kept a whole row of pipes full and ready to go.

The third mate was Flask, another Massachusetts native—a short, chubby young fellow, always ready for a fight with a whale. It was said he would toy with a whale as if it were just a big mouse. Flask was tough and steady.

Now, these three mates, Starbuck, Stubb, and Flask, were very important men. They were each in charge of a whaleboat and its crew. These whaleboats were lowered over the sides of the main ship when whales were sighted. The whaleboat crews were made up of the men who pulled the oars, and the harpooner. When the time came to attack and kill a whale, the harpooner's skill with his spear usually decided who won the battle. The men in each crew trusted one another like brothers.

Starbuck had chosen Queequeg for his harpooner. You have already heard about him. Next was Tashtego, a full-blooded Massachusetts Indian, known for his bravery and daring. Tashtego was long and lean and strong as a steel wire. Tashtego was Stubb's harpooner. The third harpooner was Daggoo, a gigantic, coal-black African. With two hoop earrings and a height of six feet and five inches, he was quite a sight next to little Flask, the mate with whom he worked.

There was another whaleboat crew on the *Pequod*, though nothing was known about them. One night before we sailed, a crew had slipped on board like shadows and disappeared into the area of Ahab's cabin. They were more like ghosts than men. The gossip was that they were Ahab's personal crew, led by a strange man named Fedallah.

The rest of the crew came in all shapes, sizes, and colors—from all over the world, especially islands. Most of the crew had spent their whole lives on the sea and were expert whalemen. Many had hidden aboard ships that had been passing their islands, and they had never returned. The whaling ship became their home, their own little island.

CHAPTER SIX

Ahab

While Ahab remained hidden in his cabin below the deck, the three mates ran the ship. Starbuck, Stubb, and Flask took their turns at keeping watch for whales as we fought our way south through a freezing wind. But as we sailed farther south, the weather began to turn warmer.

It was on a cloudy morning just before noon that Ahab finally appeared. I was on deck at the back of the ship. I looked over my shoulder and then looked again. Sure enough, there he stood. Shivers ran all through me. His skin was a dark, bronze color, and his head was a mass of long, gray hair. Winding out of his hair and right down one side of his face and neck was an ugly white scar.

I stared at this face for several moments, unable to move my eyes from it. It was only after I began to believe what I saw that I noticed the rest of him. As my eyes ran down his body, I saw that leg I had already heard about. A slender, white stump stuck out from one of Ahab's trouser legs. It was a piece of ivory taken from a whale's jaw. A hole had been drilled on each side of the ship's deck to match the size of the leg's bottom tip. Ahab's false leg rested in one of those holes as he stood there like a statue, his eyes never leaving the open seas ahead of us.

Before long, this strange-looking man turned away and disappeared into his cabin. It was several days before we would see him again, but as the days became less gloomy he came on deck more often. Still, he said not a word to the crew.

The days had become sunnier, and the night skies twinkled with a million stars. The waves caught the light from the heavens, and the water was a flashing, glittering carpet of blue and silver stretching before us.

Ahab spent some time on deck nearly every

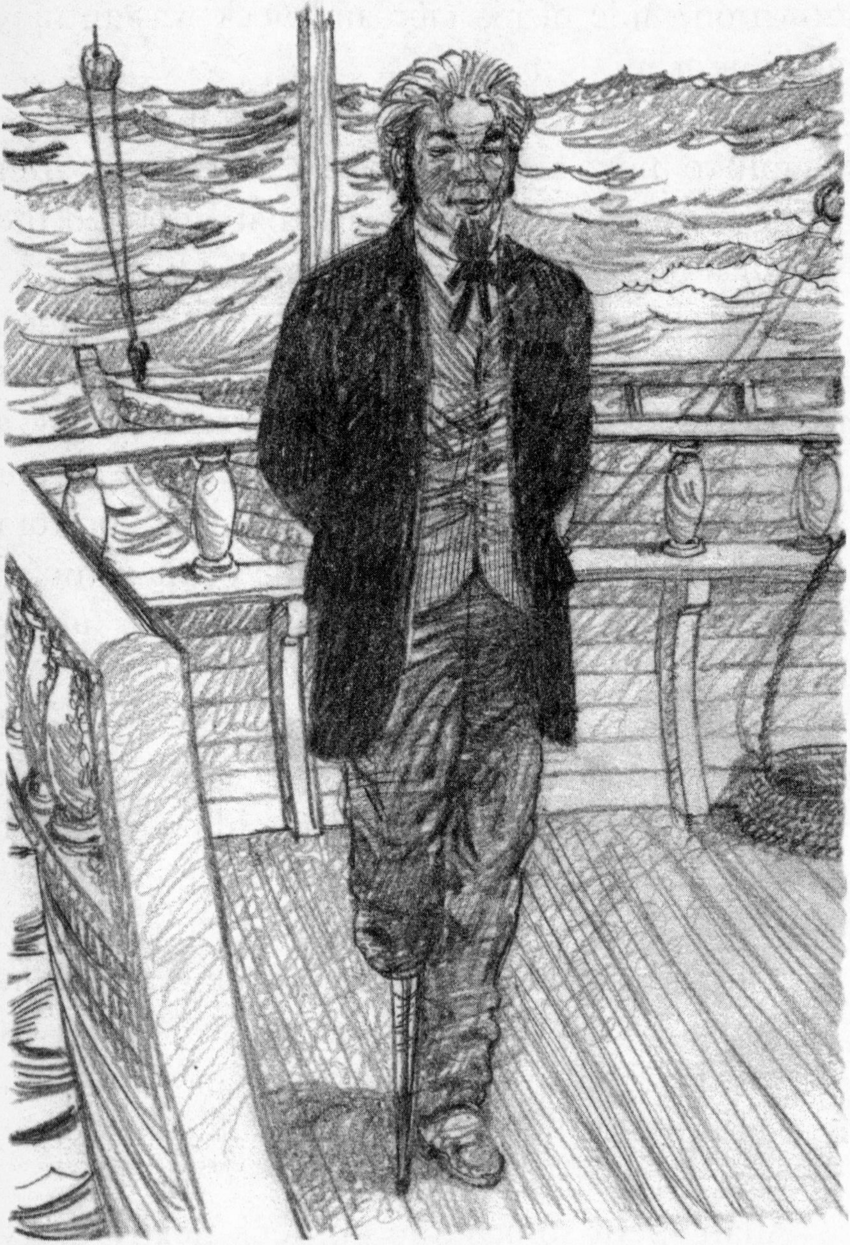

day, and most nights. The crew could hear the tapping and thumping of that ivory leg as he paced back and forth above their bunks. We began to wonder when he got any sleep, or if he slept at all.

One night, Stubb asked him to return to his cabin so the rest of us could get some sleep. Ahab became angry, called him a dog, and charged at him with a most terrible look in his eyes. Poor Stubb was scared to death and ran back to his cabin. Our captain was full of a restless anger of some kind. I thought it might be a hatred toward the whale that had chewed his leg off.

CHAPTER SEVEN

A Short Science Lesson

Before we get much deeper into our chase for the whale, I should give you a few facts about this huge beast. You need to know a little bit about what to expect, for we are coming into the whale's neighborhood now.

First, let me say that I do not agree with those scientists who call the whale a mammal. I cannot see how anything that spends its entire life in the water could be anything but a fish. And even the Bible says that the creature that swallowed Jonah was a "great fish."

I do agree that there are some differences between the whale and other fish. First, the

whale has lungs and warm blood. This means he must come to the surface of the water to fill his lungs with air and to control his temperature. When he rises to the surface to take a breath, he spits out the old air and takes in new—just like we human beings inhale and exhale through our nose and mouth. But the whale does it a little differently. He has a blowhole located in the center of his forehead. When the air blows through this hole it comes out with such force that it creates a burst of air and water, or spout. This misty spout is the first thing a whale hunter looks for as he stands watch on the deck, and it is the reason for the famous shout:

"There she blows!"

I'll mention just one more thing that one notices about whales—the broad tail. All the other fish have up-and-down (or vertical) tails. But the whale's tail lies flat. So, if you see a spouting fish with a huge, flat tail, you will have spotted a whale.

Now, among these warm-blooded, air-breathing, spouting, flat-tailed fishes, there are many types. Of these, the *Sperm Whale*, *Hump-backed Whale*, *Razor Back Whale*, and *Right*

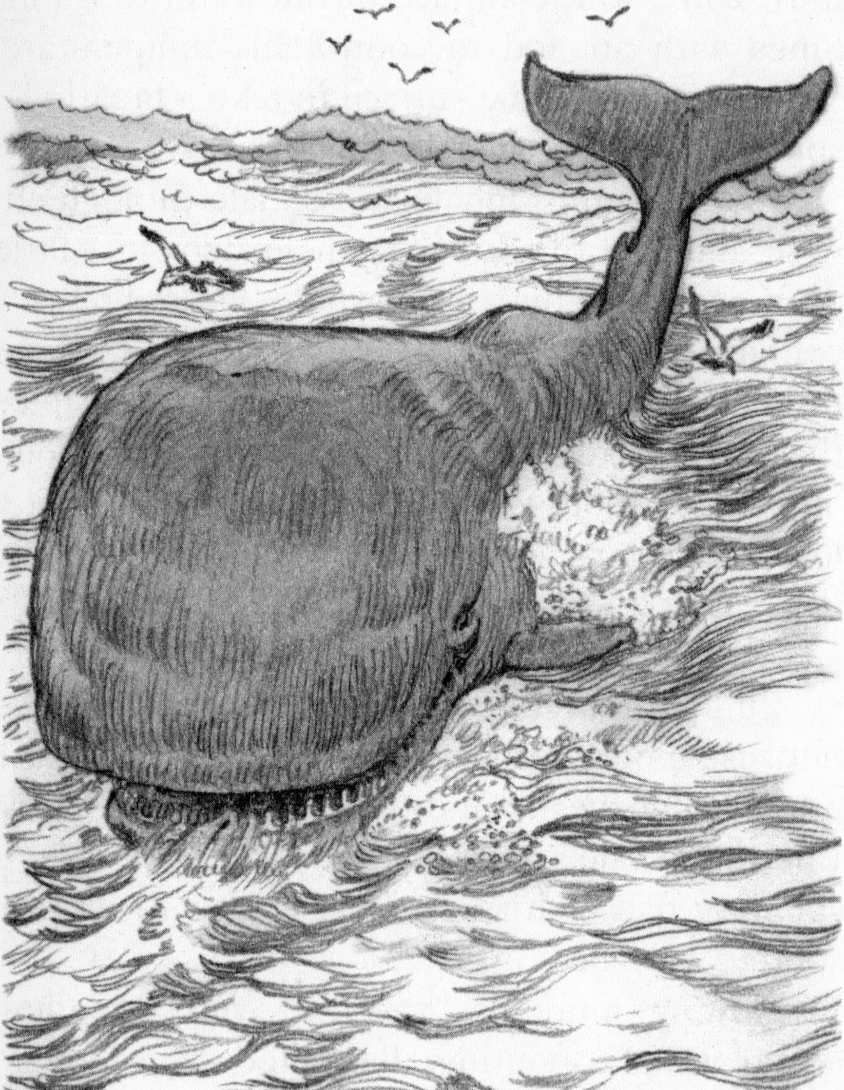

Whale are the largest and most valuable for the quality and amount of oil they contain. And of this group, the Sperm whale is the king of the fishes, just as the lion is king of the beasts. He is the hardest thing to kill, but the tons of valuable oil that come from his body make hunting him worth the danger. His oil lights the lamps around the world. The Sperm whale is also the only whale from which we get spermaceti. This precious substance is used to make expensive perfumes.

Before ending this little science lesson, I should give you some idea about the size of the whale. Many whales grow to be over ninety feet in length, and old sailors would tell you they have seen great creatures which would measure more than that! The largest of the Sperm whales weigh over ninety tons! I could go on with facts and stories, but you shall learn more about these marvelous fish as the journey continues.

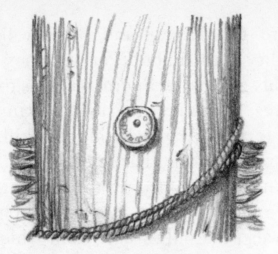

CHAPTER EIGHT

The Gold Doubloon

One evening, after pacing back and forth all day, Ahab suddenly stopped. He put his ivory leg into its hole on the deck and ordered Starbuck to send everybody to the rear of the ship's deck.

"Send everybody aft," shouted Ahab. "Men up there on the masts, come down!"

When the entire crew was in front of him, Ahab stared at them with a gleam in his eyes.

"What do ye do when ye see a whale, men?" he cried.

"Sing out for him!" shouted the crew.

"Good!" cried Ahab, with a wild sound in his voice. "And what d'ye do next, men?"

"Lower the whaleboats away, and go after him!"
"And what tune d'ye sing as ye pull the oars?"
"*A dead whale or a sunk boat!*"
"Look! Do ye see this Spanish ounce of gold? It is a sixteen-dollar piece, men, a doubloon. Do ye see it? Mr. Starbuck, hand me that yonder hammer."

While the chief mate was getting the hammer, Ahab was slowly rubbing the gold piece against his jacket, humming a strange sound that seemed to come from deep inside him. Starbuck returned and handed our captain the hammer. He then nailed the gold coin to the mast. Turning to face us he cried out:

"Whoever finds me a White Whale with a wrinkled head and a crooked jaw... Whoever first sights that White Whale with three holes in his right fin... Whoever of ye boys that first finds me that same White Whale... *he* shall have this gold piece!"

"Hurray! Hurray!" cried the seamen.

"It's a White Whale, I say," repeated Ahab, as he threw down the hammer. "A White Whale! Peel your eyes for him! Look sharp! If ye see no more than a bubble, sing out!"

"Captain Ahab," said Tashtego, "that White Whale must be the one called Moby Dick."

"Moby Dick?" shouted Ahab. "Do ye know the White Whale then, Tash?"

"And does he have a different sort of spout?" asked Daggoo.

"And does he have many harpoon on him, too, Captain?" cried Queequeg.

"Aye, harpoons all in him, Queequeg. Yes, Daggoo, his spout is a big one, and white as snow. Death and devils, men. It is Moby Dick ye have spoken of—Moby Dick!"

"Captain Ahab," said Starbuck, "I have heard of Moby Dick. But was it this Moby Dick that took off thy leg?"

"Who told you that?" cried Ahab. "Aye, Starbuck, it was Moby Dick that caused this dead stump I stand on now. Yes," he shouted bitterly, sounding like some wounded animal, "it was that cursed whale and I'll chase him around every ocean in the world before I'm done!"

Starbuck spoke up. "I am willing to chase this White Whale to the death if it means money in our pockets, but there will be little reward if all we are after is revenge upon a dumb animal. Such a hunt would be crazy and against the laws of God. Ye are not asking for our skill, Captain Ahab. Ye are asking for our lives."

Ahab went on screaming about his hatred for Moby Dick. He was like a crazy man who would

listen to no one. The three mates backed away from him as they saw that nothing would calm the storm inside Ahab's dark soul. Starbuck's face was white as chalk. He shivered and turned away. "God keep me! God keep us all!" murmured Starbuck to himself.

But Ahab did not hear him. He had already left to return to his cabin, the white ivory peg tapping, tapping, tapping across the ship's deck. A gray fog crept over the ship, but the gold doubloon still shone brightly on the mast.

CHAPTER NINE

Moby Dick

The days and weeks passed. The wind filled our sails and pulled our ship across miles and miles of the world's great oceans. I stayed busy with my sailor's tasks. There was always something to be done. As I worked with the others, whether it was scrubbing decks, mending nets, or keeping watch for whales, I kept my ears open to the stories they told. I was most interested in the tales about Moby Dick.

Much of what I heard seemed to be nothing but gossip and rumors. At the same time, some of the things must have been true because more than one sailor often repeated the same facts.

For instance, I was told that Moby Dick was larger than even the largest Sperm whales anyone had ever seen. He had a white, wrinkled forehead and a crooked lower jaw. And, according to most accounts, he carried in his side several harpoons left there by past efforts to catch him. Whether it was because of these harpoons sticking in him, or whether it was just Moby Dick's own nature, I do not know, but every sailor swore he was an angry, vicious murderer who would attack the ships and men hunting him.

These same sailors, however, also said there was a strange beauty and mystery about him. Some even said that Moby Dick had been sighted in two different oceans at the same time. It was almost as though there were things both real and unreal about him—things both good and evil. But everybody agreed on one thing: It was this whale, this Moby Dick, that had attacked Captain Ahab and chewed his leg from him.

These stories that I heard during my days stayed with me into my nights. I tossed and turned and could not sleep.

CHAPTER TEN

Our First Whale

The weeks turned into months, and still we had seen no whales. We sailed through storms that ripped at our sails and tossed our ship on waves as tall as a house. There were times when I was sure we would be swamped with water or thrown over the side. Then, there were other days when the wind was so calm that there was barely enough in the sails to move us along. I hoped and prayed that Captain Ahab knew where we were and where the whales were.

On one of those calm days, I was on deck with Queequeg helping to weave a mat. The sky was completely clouded over, and the air was hot and damp. In and out, in and out, I weaved the straw. I was lost in a daydream when a strange, musical cry shook me.

"There she blows! She blows! There she blows! About two miles! A whole school of 'em!" Tashtego called from his lookout watch on top of the mast.

All at once, the whole ship jumped into action. Tashtego had spotted whales!

My heart was racing. My first whale! I rushed to the side of the ship along with the others. This was the moment I had been waiting for!

At Ahab's command, the mates, along with their harpooners and crews, leaped to the rails, ready to lower their whaleboats into the water. The rest of the crew ran in all directions. Each harpooner had grabbed his spear and looked as though he could not wait to begin the chase.

Suddenly, all eyes left the whales and stared at Ahab. He was surrounded by five dark phantoms that seemed to have come out of the air. They flitted to the other side of the deck and, without a sound, lowered a boat that hung there. The rest of us had thought this was a spare boat, but we now saw that it was for Ahab. A tall, dark figure stood in the front of the boat. He was dressed all in black, and his white hair was twisted and coiled up into a white turban.

This was Ahab's private crew. Ahab must have hidden them in his cabin until just the right time. We had heard whispers about this phantom crew. Now they were above decks for the first time and leaping into Ahab's boat.

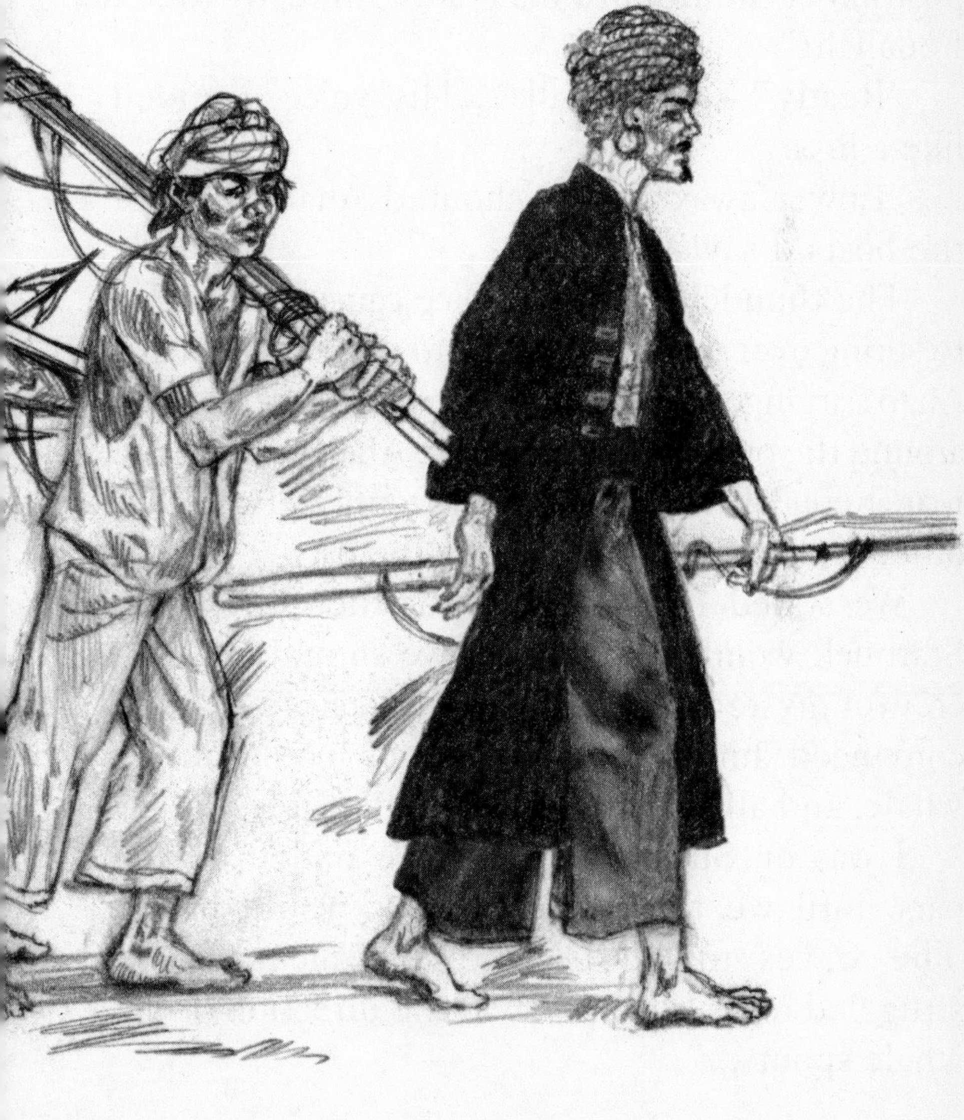

While the rest of us were still trying to understand what was happening, Ahab cried out to the dark figure standing in the harpooner's position at the front of his boat, "All ready there, Fedallah?"

"Ready," said Fedallah. His voice sounded like a hiss.

"Lower away then," shouted Ahab. "Lower the boats, I say!"

The thunder in Ahab's voice caused the crews to spring over the ship's side into the tossing boats. Ahab's strange crew appeared in their boat, coming around the other end of the ship. Ahab stood at the rear. Fedallah was perched in front, and the four other mysterious men pulled at the oars.

We stared for a moment at the eerie crew. Starbuck wondered whether we should join this crew of mysterious devils. Finally, carefree Stubb convinced him that even devils could kill a whale, and all four boats began the chase.

I was on Starbuck's crew. We pulled on the oars until we thought our backs would break. The waves tossed us like toothpicks as we struggled to make our way in the direction of the whale spouts.

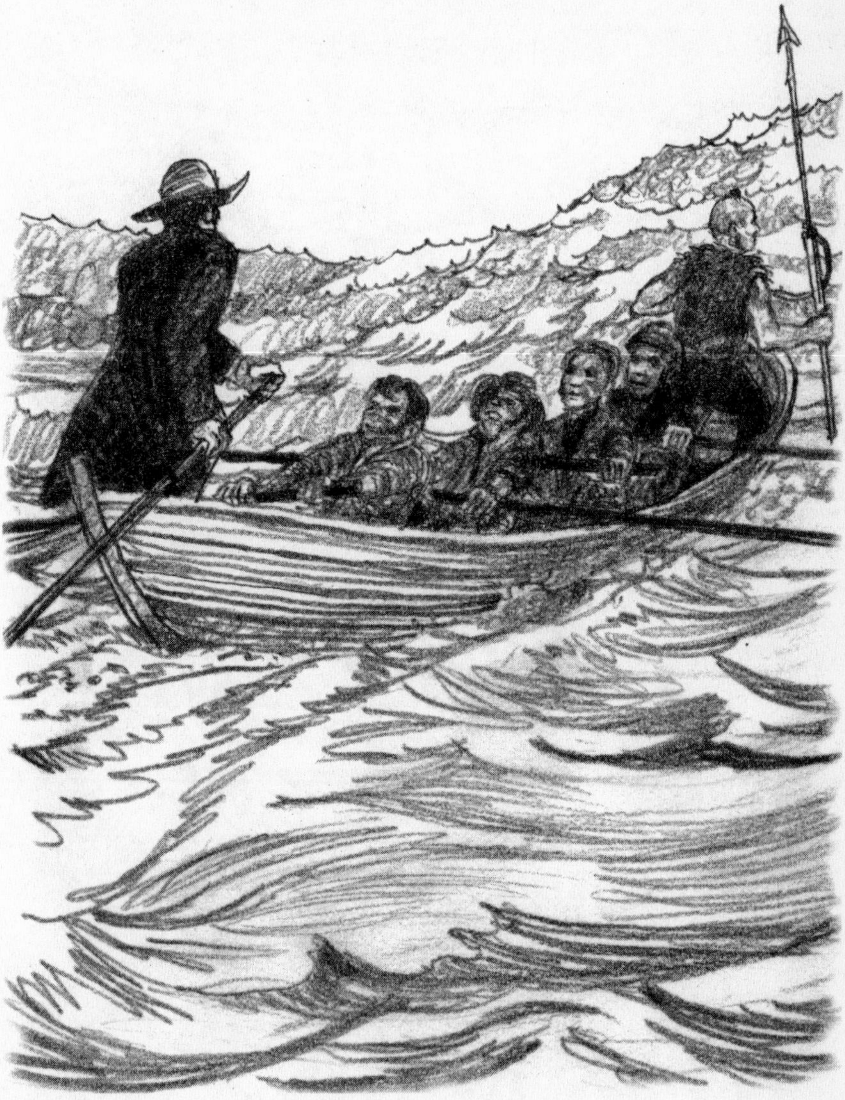

"Pull harder! Faster to the whale! Break your backs, you dogs!" cried Ahab.

I had never in my life been through anything like this. My back and neck ached, and I thought I could pull no harder on the oars without ripping my arms off. The waves curled and licked around us as we followed the spouts of mist coming from the whales. Then the clouds grew darker, and we lost sight of the other boats. The salty spray rushed into my eyes until they burned like fire. The storm grew worse, and the mist turned into a thick fog.

I could hear the voices of the other mates shouting at their crews to row harder and fight on through the waves. The voices became fainter as the boats were pulled further apart. Even the *Pequod* had disappeared from sight.

"Hang on, men," whispered Starbuck. "There is still time to kill a fish before the rain comes. There's white water again! Jump! Spring! Stand up, Queequeg!

There was a moment of silence. Then: "That's his hump. There, there, give it to him," ordered Starbuck.

A short, whistling sound filled my ears as Queequeg's harpoon flew through the air. Then, all at once, the whale rose beneath us like an earthquake and a giant wave crashed over us from behind. Our boat was lifted out of the water like a toy. A rush of hot mist shot up from the whale's head as it rolled and tumbled under the boat. The next thing I knew, the whole crew was flying through the air and into the churning water. To make things even worse, the whale had escaped. Queequeg's harpoon had only angered him.

Heads began bobbing to the surface. By some miracle, we were all alive. We began swimming toward our boat, picking up our oars as we went. We tumbled back into the boat, and there we sat, up to our knees in water that had flooded in.

The wind began to howl and the storm roared and snapped around us like a lion. We shouted out, but there was no answer. The sky grew darker with the shadows of night, and still there was no sign of our ship. Starbuck dug around in the waterproof sack tied to the boat and found some dry matches. He lit the boat's lantern and told Queequeg to hold it up like a tiny lighthouse.

By morning, we were running out of hope. The fog still spread over the sea. Suddenly, Queequeg jumped to his feet, holding his hand to his ear. We all heard a faint creaking. Then we saw our ship about to run over us. We jumped overboard just before our boat disappeared under the *Pequod*.

I was the last to be pulled from the sea. I lay on the deck, thanking God to be alive. I learned that Stubb and Flask had harpooned a whale, but they had to cut it loose because of the storm. The strange thing to me was that no one was upset. They acted as though this was all part of the job of whaling. I had great respect for their courage in the face of death.

CHAPTER ELEVEN

The Mysterious Spout

The next day and the next week brought smooth sailing. We had passed by a famous whaling area off the coast of Africa, but not a spout had we seen. On we went toward the tip of Africa and the Cape of Good Hope.

One peaceful and moonlit night a silvery jet rose up far in front of the ship. Fedallah was the first to see it. His weird cry rang out. "There she blows!"

Every sleeping sailor leaped from his bed. Ahab flew from his cabin. The rapid tapping of his dead stump sounded like nails being hammered into a coffin. He ordered a sharp watch, but the mysterious spout was seen no more that night.

Some days later, at the same, silent midnight hour, it returned. Again, all swore they saw it, but as soon as we turned to chase it, it was gone as if it had never been there.

The same thing happened for the next few nights. We could never catch this ghost. It was as if a spirit were tempting us, pulling us toward it.

There are many mysteries in this world that can never be explained. I thought Fedallah might know the meaning of the mysterious spout, but that strange man said nothing.

CHAPTER TWELVE

The Squid

As we entered the Indian Ocean, a gentle, peaceful air settled upon us. The breezes filling our sails made our masts look like three palm trees bending softly back and forth.

One clear, blue morning, Daggoo saw a frightening sight as he kept his watch on the top of the main mast. In the distance, a great white shape rose to the top of the water and shone before our ship like a huge drift of snow. The glistening thing stayed on the surface for a short time, then sank slowly from sight. Silently, it came up again. Daggoo could not be sure what he was seeing. It didn't look like a whale, but could it be Moby Dick?

Again the weird shape went down, but the next time it rose Daggoo screamed, "There! There again! She rises! Right ahead!"

The seamen rushed to their positions on deck like a swarm of bees. Ahab stood on the bow ready to bark his orders and stared in the direction of Daggoo's outstretched arm. As soon as he caught sight of the white hulk, he gave orders to lower all the boats.

The four boats were soon on the water, all pulling toward the object in the water. Suddenly it went down, and just as suddenly came back. For a few moments we forgot about Moby Dick and stared at the most amazing of all the things that hide in the secret seas. A giant, jellylike mass, creamy in color, lay floating on the water. Long arms reached out from its center, curling and twisting like a nest of snakes. It seemed to have no face, or none we could see.

With a low sucking sound it slowly disappeared again. Starbuck, still staring at the boiling water where it had sunk, shrieked with a wild voice, "I would almost rather have seen Moby Dick and fought him than to have seen thee, thou white ghost!"

"What was it, sir?" said Flask.

"The great live squid," said Starbuck quietly. "They say that not many whale hunters who see the beast ever return to tell about it."

But Ahab said nothing. Turning his boat, he returned to the ship. The other boats followed silently behind him.

There are plenty of tales and superstitions about the squid. Some say it is the largest creature in the sea. It is so seldom seen, however, that there are very few facts to pass on. It is true that some whales' bellies have held arms of this monster which were thirty feet long! It is also believed that of all the types of whales, only the Sperm whale eats the squid as his only source of food.

I wasn't sure what to believe about the squid, but what Starbuck had said made me wonder whether any of us would set foot on land again. Queequeg had a happier way of looking at it.

"When you see him squid," he said, sharpening his harpoon to a razor's edge, "then you quick see him Sperm whale."

CHAPTER THIRTEEN

Stubb Kills a Whale

The next day was warm and still. I was keeping watch on top of the masthead while my mind wandered and dreamed of things far away. As I swayed back and forth with the gentle rocking of the mast, I soon became sleepy. The whole crew was lazy on that quiet afternoon.

Suddenly, a bursting of bubbles from the water below me brought me back to life. I was so surprised that I had to grab the sail lines and hang on for dear life. When I got over my shock and looked below, the sight almost took my breath away. Close below me, not more than a hundred yards away, a giant Sperm whale lay rolling in the water. His broad back shone in the sun like a mirror. He looked like a big silver ship. In a split second, our sleepy ship was awake. Cries burst from all three masts. The familiar call, "There she blows!" rang across the decks. Below us, the great fish kept up its lazy rolling. Every so often it sent a sparkling, misty spout into the air.

"Clear away the boats! Prepare to lower!" Ahab cried.

The noise and shouting of the crew must have scared the whale. He began moving slowly away. We paddled our boats as quietly as possible, but as we got near, the monster threw his broad tail forty feet straight up in the air and dove out of sight.

"There he dives!" was the cry. We knew we had nothing to do now but wait for the whale to come to the surface. To my surprise, Stubb sat back and lit his pipe.

After a short time, the whale shot up directly in front of Stubb's boat. Stubb decided that this was his whale to kill. Still puffing on his pipe, Stubb cheered his crew on.

"Give it all you've got, my men! But keep cool. Pull with long, strong strokes but be cool as

cucumbers. Be ready there, Tashtego. Stand up and be ready!"

"Hook-ah! Snook-ah!" screamed the Indian harpooner. "Hi-badee! Catch 'em all!"

The crew pulled together. They came closer and closer to the whale. When they were nearly on top of him, Stubb shouted, "Give it to him, Tash! Give it to him!"

Tashtego's harpoon sailed through the air straight into the whale. The whale dove, taking the harpoon with it. Finally, after pulling the boat behind it on a wild, crashing ride, the whale slowed. "Haul in! Haul in!" cried Stubb. The crew began pulling the line in, bringing the boat right next to the huge whale. Stubb planted his feet as firmly as he could and threw spear after spear into the whale.

The puffs of steamy mist coming from the whale's spout hole grew smaller. The puffs of smoke from Stubb's pipe seemed to come twice as fast. The battle was nearly over.

The water was a bubbling pool of red foam. Stubb ordered his crew to pull up beside the whale. As the boat came within a few feet of the wounded giant, Stubb drove one last spear deep into the area of its heart. With one last great rush of spray, the whale rolled on its side and lay still in the water.

"He's dead, Mr. Stubb," said Tashtego.

The thrill of the hunt was over, but there was some long, hard work ahead for all of us. Stubb's whale had been killed a long distance from the ship. This made the job of getting the huge fish pulled in even harder.

Ahab's crew had returned to the ship. We tied the other three boats together in a line and began towing our prize to the ship. Eighteen men and thirty-six arms worked together hour after hour, tugging and hauling the great fish toward the ship. Sometimes it seemed as though we moved just an inch at a time.

Darkness came. Lanterns hanging from the *Pequod* guided us. The oarsmen, their backs and arms aching and burning, continued to struggle and pull. Captain Ahab hung a final lantern on the ship's side. His eyes had an empty, hollow look as he stared at the dead whale. Although we had killed a whale, he seemed sad and angry. It was as if he could never be happy until Moby Dick had been killed—that great beast that had

stolen his leg. We could kill a thousand whales, but until the White Whale was dead, Ahab would find no peace.

Unlike Ahab, Stubb was so happy and excited we couldn't get him to calm down. He laughed and made jokes with the crew. He asked the cook to prepare him a feast of whale steak to celebrate the victory. Daggoo leaped over the side and cut a slab of meat from the whale. The cook then made it exactly as Stubb wanted. When he had stuffed himself, Stubb lit his pipe and leaned back in his chair.

Around midnight, we went below decks to our bunks. But we didn't sleep much. Stubb was not the only one that night to have a late bite of whale meat.

Thousands of sharks began to circle the ship and move in for their own feast. You could hear their tails smack and snap against the ship's sides. They were fighting each other for a place at their own supper table. When the sharks finally left, I closed my eyes and drifted off to sleep. As it turned out, I would need all the rest I could get. There was still a lot of work ahead before there would be whale oil in our barrels.

CHAPTER FOURTEEN

Cutting Up

The following day was Sunday. Back on land, shops and factories were closed and people were in church. Things were quite different on a whaling ship if a huge whale hung there waiting to be cut up. No, there would be no rest on this Sunday.

As I said before, the reason men hunt whales is to get the oil from their bodies. Most of the oil comes from the outside part of the whale. Just under the whale's skin there is a thick layer of fat called blubber. This blubber is as much as fifteen inches thick. When it is boiled and melted, the oil comes out and is collected and stored in barrels in the bottom of the ship. When the ship returns home, the owners of the ship sell the oil. There might be as much as fifty barrels of oil taken from just one whale. But it takes a huge amount of work to get a fish that weighs ninety tons into fifty barrels!

One end of a rope was tied to the ship and the other end to a man. The man was lowered onto the whale and began cutting strips of blubber from its body. It was almost like peeling the skin from an orange. After a strip was cut loose, a huge hook (itself weighing as much as a hundred pounds) was used to lift the blubber to the deck of the ship. There, the strips were cut into smaller pieces that would fit into the boiling pots. Up and down went the hook. The men pulling the ropes were completely tired out by the time the work was done. It had taken the whole morning.

The one last job was to remove the head of the whale. Deep inside the Sperm whale's head is the valuable stuff known as spermaceti, used to make expensive perfumes. The Sperm whale's head is about twenty-five feet long. You can imagine how heavy it must be! It would have tipped our boat over had we tried to lift it over the side of the ship, as we had lifted the pieces of blubber.

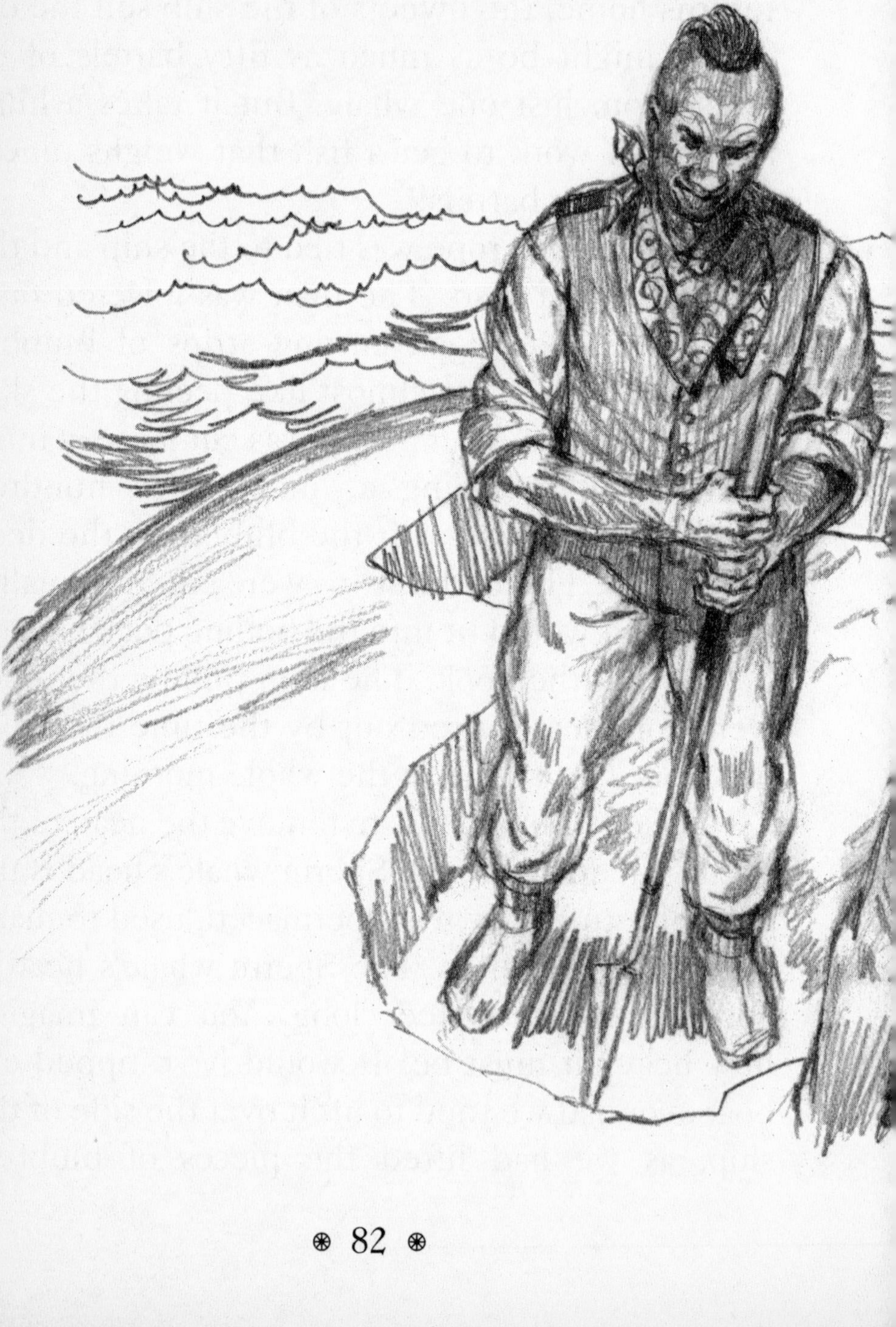

Instead, once it had been cut from the rest of the body, the head was pulled just out of the water and hung to the outside of the ship. Later, the spermaceti could be dug from its very center.

When all the work was done, Ahab shouted out, "Haul in the chains! Cut the rest of the whale loose from the ship!"

The peeled skeleton was released and began to float into the distance. Shrieking sea birds swooped down and tore away scraps of skin. Sharks swarmed around, as they fought for one last vicious bite at what was left of this proud beast.

It was noon, and the crew went below for their dinner. The deck was quiet, and the sea was calm. Captain Ahab came out of his cabin. After he had taken a short walk around the deck, he stopped to stare over the side at the whale's head. He looked intently into its dead eyes.

"Speak, ye giant, mysterious head. Speak, and tell me the secrets you hide about the seas. Tell me everything ye know. But now I see ye cannot talk. Ye hold the secrets to which I long to know the answers, but ye cannot speak a single word. Ye cannot tell me what I need to know."

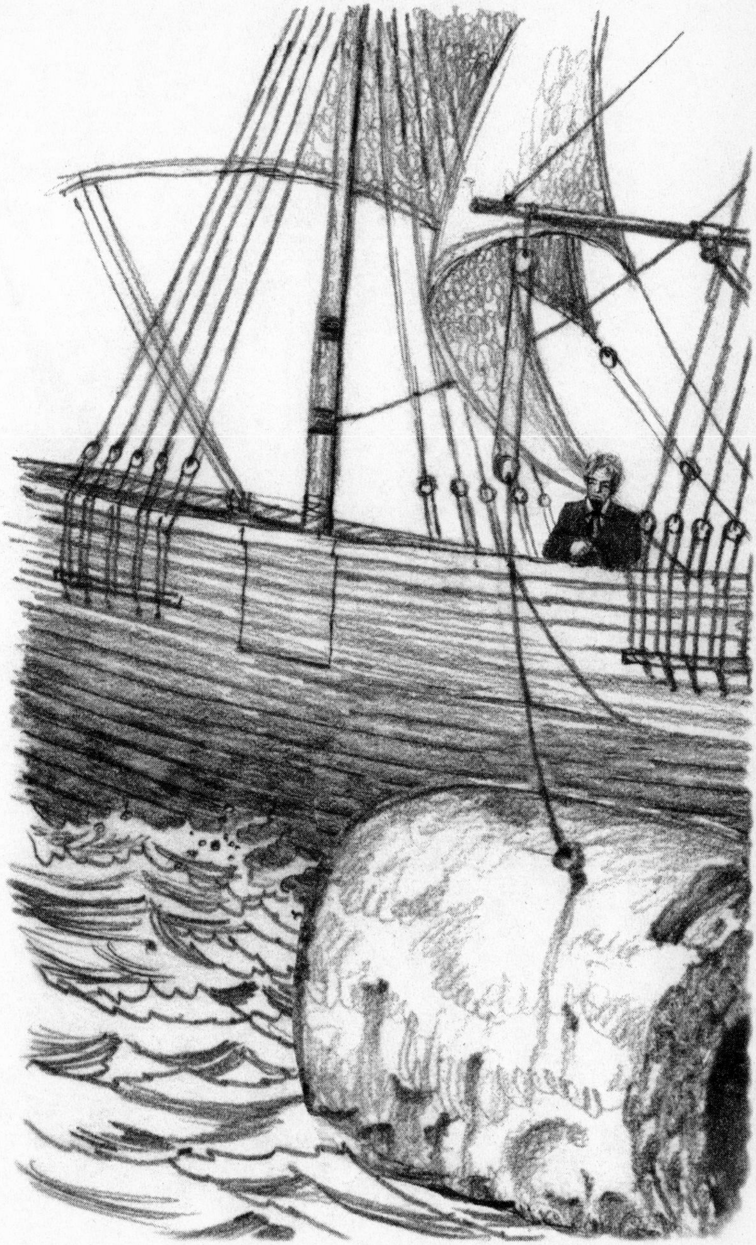

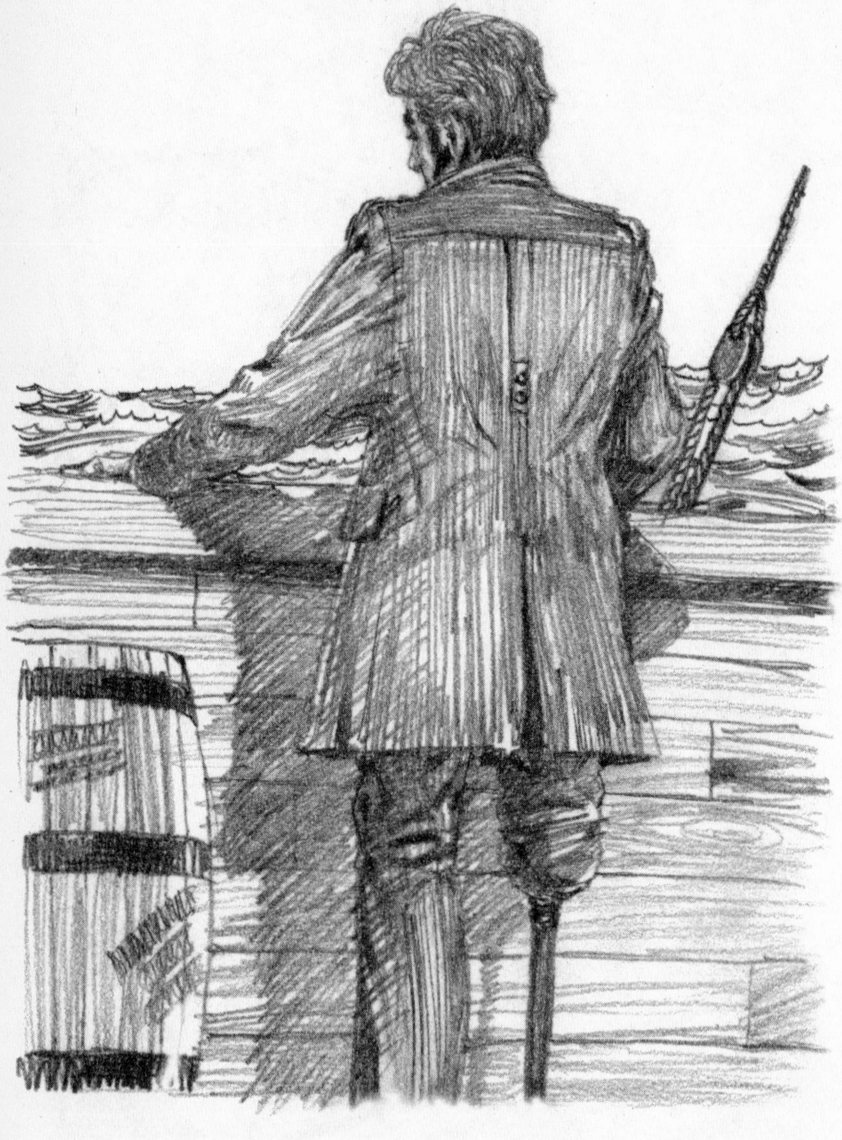

Ahab's strange talk was ended by a cry from the mast above. "Sail ho!" cried the voice. "Sail ho! A ship ahead!"

"Aye? Well, now, that's cheerful news. If this dead whale will tell me nothing, perhaps there's news of Moby Dick on this ship."

As soon as the other ship came near, Ahab cried, "Have ye seen the White Whale?"

CHAPTER FIFTEEN

The *Jeroboam*

Captain Mayhew of the *Jeroboam* gave us some bad news. It seemed that not long after the crew of the *Jeroboam* had left home, they met a ship that warned them of the dangers of hunting Moby Dick. In spite of this, a year or two later, upon sighting Moby Dick, Captain Mayhew's chief mate, Macey, burned with desire to attack him.

Mayhew, ignoring the warnings, agreed to let Macey lower a boat. Macey talked five other men into going with him, and after a hard chase they were able to get one harpoon into the whale. But then the monstrous white hump rose from beneath Macey's boat. As the horrified crew

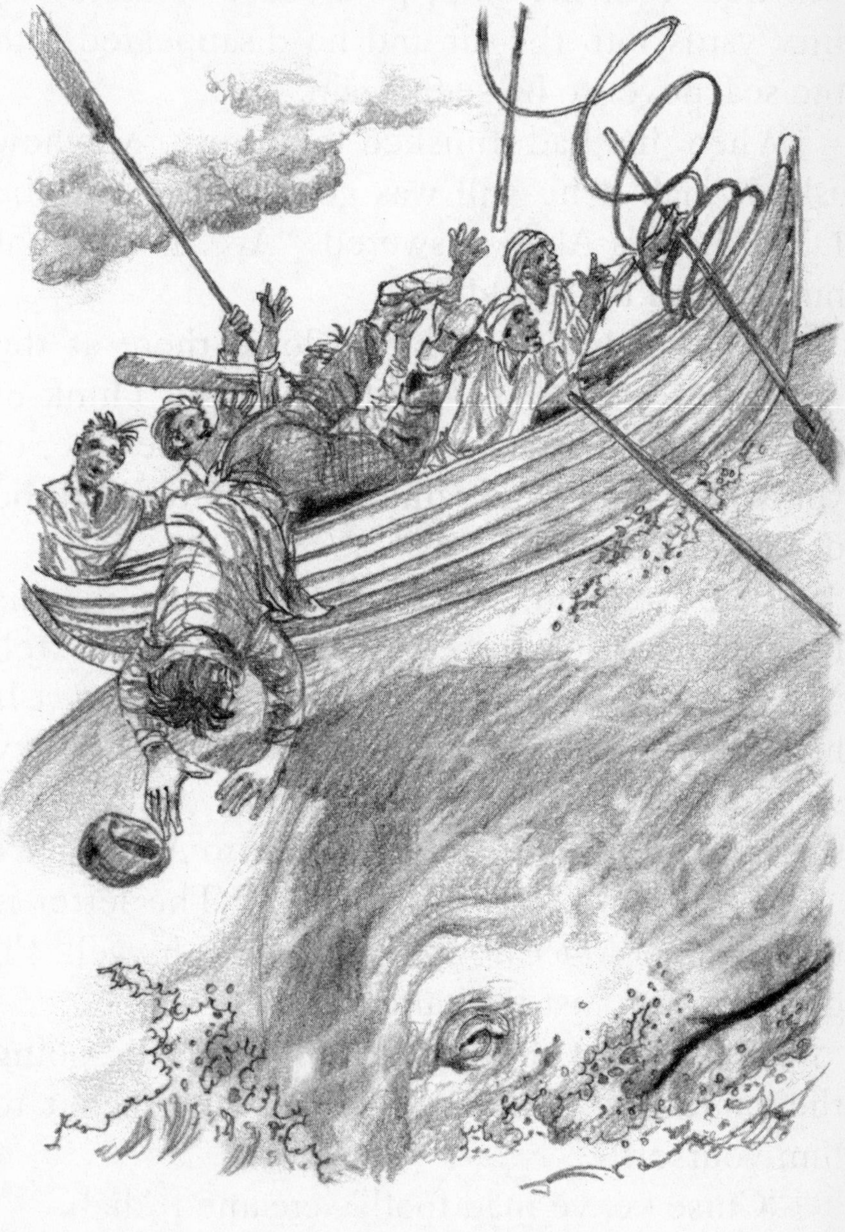

watched from the ship, poor Macey was tossed fifty yards into the air and he disappeared into the sea, never to be seen again.

When he had finished his story, Mayhew asked Ahab if he still was going to hunt Moby Dick. To this Ahab answered, "Aye. I will hunt him around the world!"

"Think, think of Macey down there at the bottom of the ocean!" said Mayhew. "Think of that man who attacked Moby Dick. Beware, or you will come to the same end. You, too, will be dead and lost to the sea."

Ahab sneered, with no comment on this frightening tale. Instead, he went on to tell Mayhew that he had a letter for the *Jeroboam*. It had been given to him to deliver in case they should meet. Starbuck went below deck to get the letter, returned, and handed it to Ahab.

"Well, look here," Ahab said. "The letter is for that poor Macey. And he's dead. Ah, well. I'll give it to you just the same."

"Nay! Keep the letter. You'll soon be going the same way as Macey. You can deliver it to him yourself!"

"Curse ye, ye mad fool!" screamed Ahab.

The two ships parted, and the sails of the *Jeroboam* became a faint speck in the distance.

I shuddered at what I had heard. The stories about the White Whale were true. Moby Dick was a killer!

CHAPTER SIXTEEN

Stubb and Flask Kill a Right Whale

Not many days after meeting the *Jeroboam*, a school of Right whales was sighted. The Right whale is not as valuable as the Sperm whale, but Ahab told Stubb and Flask to attack. Within a short time, both crews had harpoons in one of the whales.

I watched from the deck as the whale swam in circles around the ship, towing the two boats behind him. After some deep dives and a fierce fight, the whale gave up and lay floating near the ship. Hundreds of sharks soon began to circle, but before they could do much damage we had the whale alongside.

When the blubber had been stripped and loaded, the Right whale's head was removed and hung on the ship's side opposite from the head of the Sperm whale still hanging there.

As the crew continued working, Stubb and Flask stood looking at the Right whale's head. I heard Stubb tell Flask that the only reason we had bothered to kill such a whale was to make Fedallah happy. Stubb said he had heard Fedallah whispering to Ahab. The next thing he knew, Ahab had agreed to kill the Right whale and hang its head on the ship for good luck.

Stubb had never heard of such a thing in all his years at sea. He told Flask that this strange Fedallah would bring no good luck at all. Stubb thought Fedallah was a devil who had Ahab under his control.

I wished I had not heard the two mates. I was a happy man when I left home. I had been ready to face the dangers of the sea and the risks in hunting great whales. I had never thought I would have a crazy captain who took advice from some evil, devilish harpooner.

I turned away from Stubb and Flask and saw Fedallah staring at the whales' heads. Just in front of Fedallah stood Ahab so that Fedallah was in his shadow. Wherever Ahab moved, his shadow took Fedallah with it.

Day turned to dusk, and dusk turned to night. Our ship sailed on, balanced on either side by whale heads. I wished that Ahab's mind were more balanced.

CHAPTER SEVENTEEN

A Milky Bath

The next morning, with no whales in sight to hunt, it came time to dig into the mammoth head of the Sperm whale and pull out the valuable spermaceti.

The head of the Sperm whale has two parts. The huge mouth and jaw make up the lower half. The upper half is a shell of bone and muscle. Inside that shell is what is called the whale's case. It is like one huge barrel. In a large whale, such as the one we had killed, there could be as much as five hundred gallons of spermaceti.

Once the jaw was cut loose, the harpooners became dentists. Queequeg, Daggoo, and

Tashtego carefully pulled each and every ivory tooth. There are usually forty-two in all. The rest of the jaw was cut into pieces of bone and stored below. The bone and teeth would be made into beautiful carvings and sold in shops all over the world. Now that the dental work was done, it was time to get at the top part of the head still hanging from the ship.

Nimble as a cat, Tashtego climbed up the mast and out onto one of the cross arms until he was directly above the whale's head. Then he lowered himself hand-over-hand down a rope that he had looped over the cross arm. When he was standing on that slippery, rocking head, he asked for his sharp cutting spear and began to search for the exact spot to begin breaking into the head. As carefully as a treasure hunter, he cut a hole in the head.

A bucket with a line attached to it was lowered to him. The other end of the line was held tightly by men on the deck above. Tashtego dropped the bucket down through the hole he had cut in the head. When he raised it, it was full of a bubbling, milky liquid. The bucket was pulled up to the deck, emptied in a large tub, and sent back down to Tashtego. On and on the work went. Several tubs had been filled with the sweet-smelling liquid, and the hole in the whale's head was now over twenty feet deep. Then a strange accident happened.

Whether it was that wild Indian's carelessness or the slippery, oozy surface on which Tashtego stood, we never knew—but all of a sudden, poor Tashtego fell head-first into the hole. With a horrible, oily gurgling, he went out of sight!

"Man overboard!" cried Daggoo. "Swing the bucket over to me!" Putting one foot into the bucket, and holding the line with his hands to steady himself, he shouted at us to lower him to the top of the whale's head. Still hanging just above the whale, he rammed the bucket down into the hole in the whale's head, hoping Tashtego might grab it.

"In heaven's name, man," cried Stubb, "are you trying to kill the man? How will that help him, jamming that iron bucket on top of his head? Avast! Back off! Stop!"

At that instant, the hooks holding the head to the boat tore loose. With a thunderous boom, the giant head crashed into the sea. This left poor

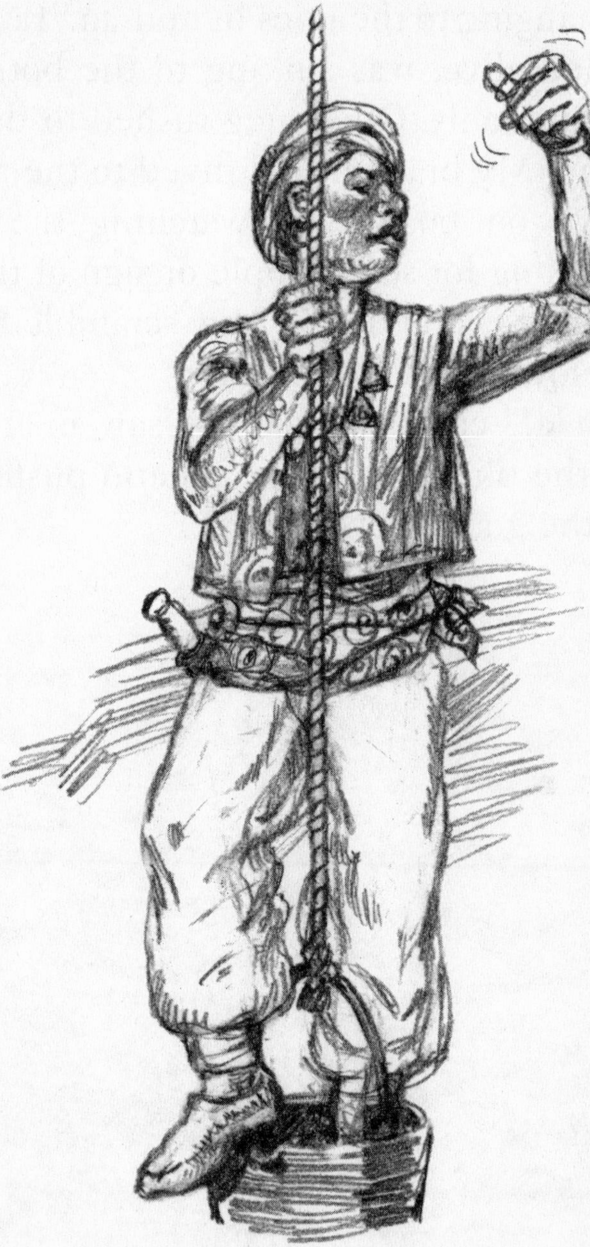

Daggoo hanging to the lines in mid-air. Tashtego, now buried alive, was sinking to the bottom of the sea. Suddenly, Queequeg rushed to the side of the ship. My brave friend dived to the rescue. Every eye on board was watching the water below, looking for some ripple or sign of the two harpooners. Several of the crew scrambled into a boat and lowered it to the water.

"Ha! Ha!" cried Daggoo. We saw an arm pop up from the blue waters like an arm pushing up through the grass above a grave.

"Both! Both! It's both of them!" yelled Daggoo with a joyful shout. Queequeg appeared, swimming with one hand and holding Tashtego's long hair with the other. Both men were pulled into the waiting boat and quickly brought up to the deck. It took some time before Tashtego opened his eyes. Queequeg lay beside his friend, too tired to move.

I fell asleep that evening thinking of Queequeg's courage and the goodness that must be in his heart. Captain Ahab had not done a thing to help save Tashtego. Instead, it was the tall savage from the islands of the Pacific whose mercy and daring gave new life to this Indian from Massachusetts. I decided there were good men all around this great world, men who could care about each other.

CHAPTER EIGHTEEN

The Grand Army

With a fair, fresh wind, the *Pequod* sailed on. We approached the strait of Sundra which passes between the islands of Sumatra and Java. Here we would leave the Indian Ocean and enter the China Seas. This was the gateway to the riches and mysteries of an oriental world, full of spices, silks, jewels, gold, and ivory.

It was Ahab's plan to go from here, past the Philippine Islands, and into the seas of Japan. On this course, we would pass through waters known to have great numbers of Sperm whales. It was also the route that Ahab thought would take us to seas where Moby Dick had most often been seen.

Sometimes in this area, Sperm whales get together in herds—as if the whales have had *enough* of being chased through four oceans and decided to join up in one big army. Some old sailors said that it sometimes looked as though there were a thousand or more spouts at one time. So the lookouts were ordered to keep a sharp eye. The soft, green palm trees waved and bowed to us from the island off our right side, and the crisp smell of cinnamon filled the air. It was a peaceful paradise. Shouts from the lookouts ended the quiet peace.

Straight ahead of our ship a great army of whales was shooting more sparkling spouts into the air than most men would see in their whole lives. They were the tall, single bursts of Sperm whales. The sea looked like a whole city of cheerful chimneys on a cold morning.

We increased our speed and started the chase. The harpooners and the rest of the crews were scrambling to their boats. Loud cheers went up. It looked as though we had a chance to capture several whales. Maybe Moby Dick himself would be among them!

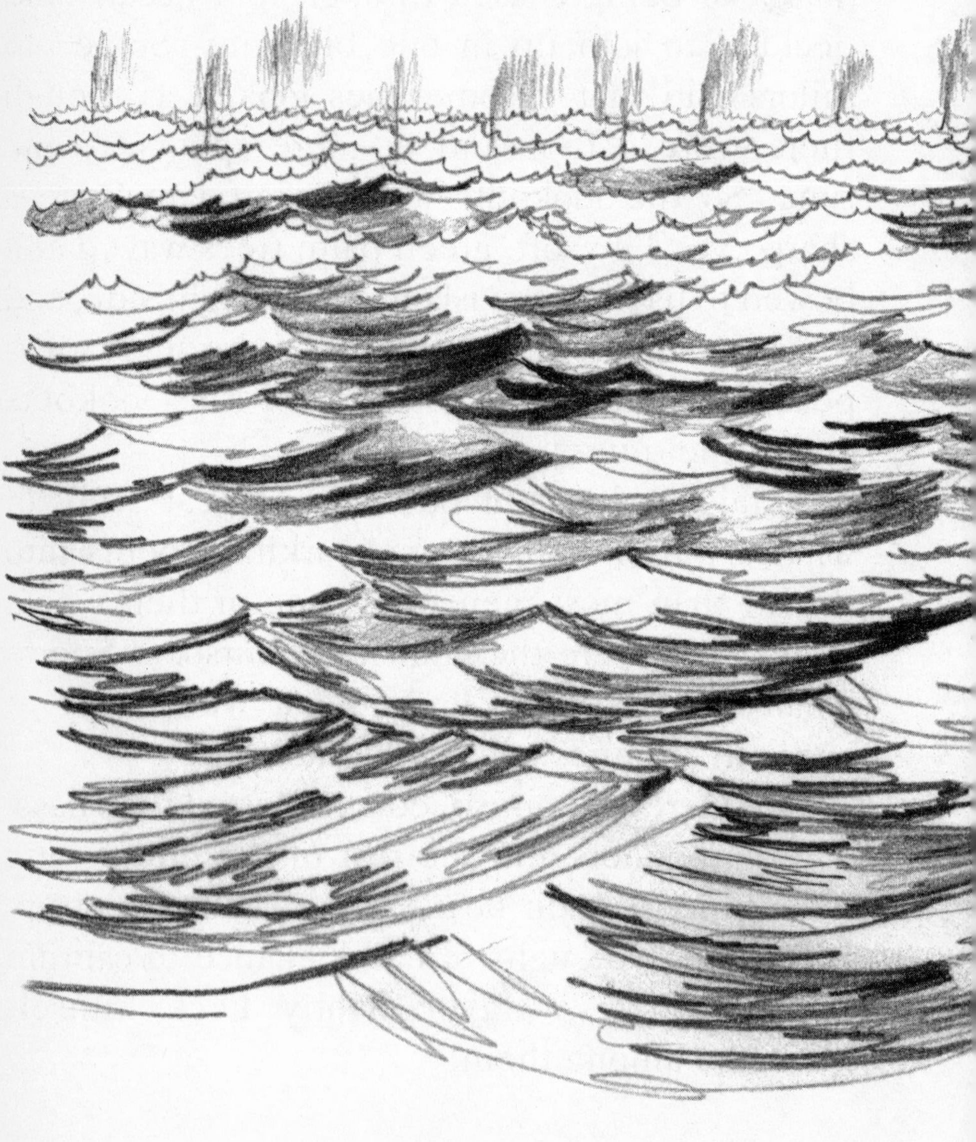

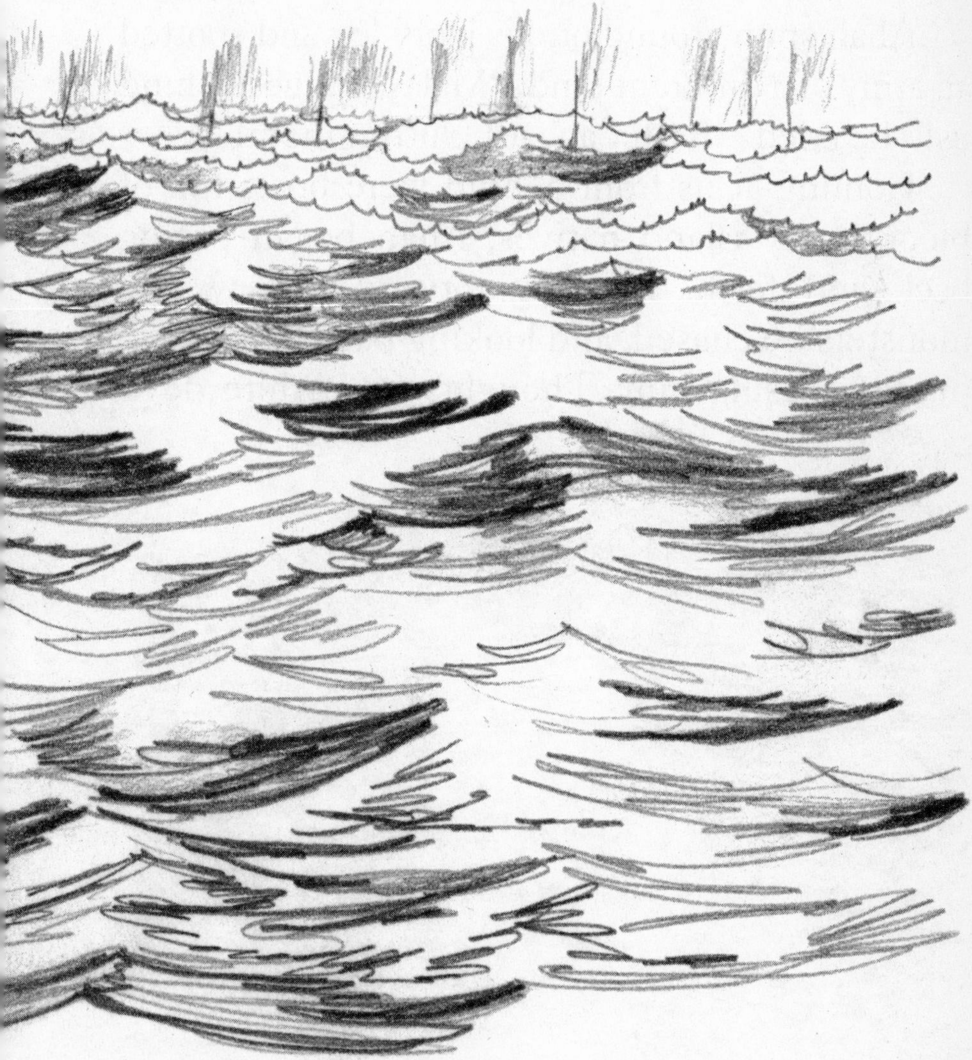

Just when our luck seemed to be getting better, Tashtego suddenly began shouting and pointing to something behind us.

Ahab spun around on his ivory leg and spotted an army of a different kind. "Malay savages behind us!" he cried. "Faster ahead! Outrun them!"

Coming at us from behind were boats full of bloodthirsty island natives. Ahab began pacing back and forth. Looking forward he saw the monsters he chased, and looking back he saw the pirates chasing him. Thoughts of a white devil

ahead of him and the dark devils behind him were more than his mind could stand. A black look came into his eyes, and the white leg tapped more quickly.

In the end we were lucky. A wind came up that increased our speed and left the pirates falling behind. We turned our eyes to the whales ahead. We were pulling nearer to them, and orders were given to lower the boats. As soon as the boats were in the water, the whales, as if they knew we were after them, began increasing their speed.

Stripped to our undershirts, we pulled the oars until it felt as though our arms would drop off. After several hours of back-breaking rowing, the whales slowed down and began to break into smaller groups. They were swimming in slow circles directly in front of us. Queequeg was the first to send his harpoon flying into one of the whales.

The instant Queequeg's harpoon was in him, the whale began thrashing and turning. His spout threw a burst of spray in our faces. His great tail, which I could see was nearly twenty feet wide, churned the water around us. Soon we were being pulled along behind the whale, right through the whole herd of whales that were around us on every side. The harpoon lines became knotted and snarled together in the bottom of the boat. As the whales rolled and slid over one another trying to break free, the lines began to wrap around their bodies. Before long, we saw that the only way out of the mess we were in was to cut the lines and release the whales.

As it turned out, after all the hard work and danger, our three boats captured just one whale in all. Flask had killed a whale early in the chase. Otherwise, we would have come away empty-handed.

There is an old saying in this business—the more whales, the less fish. I knew what that meant now—the more whales, the less you catch.

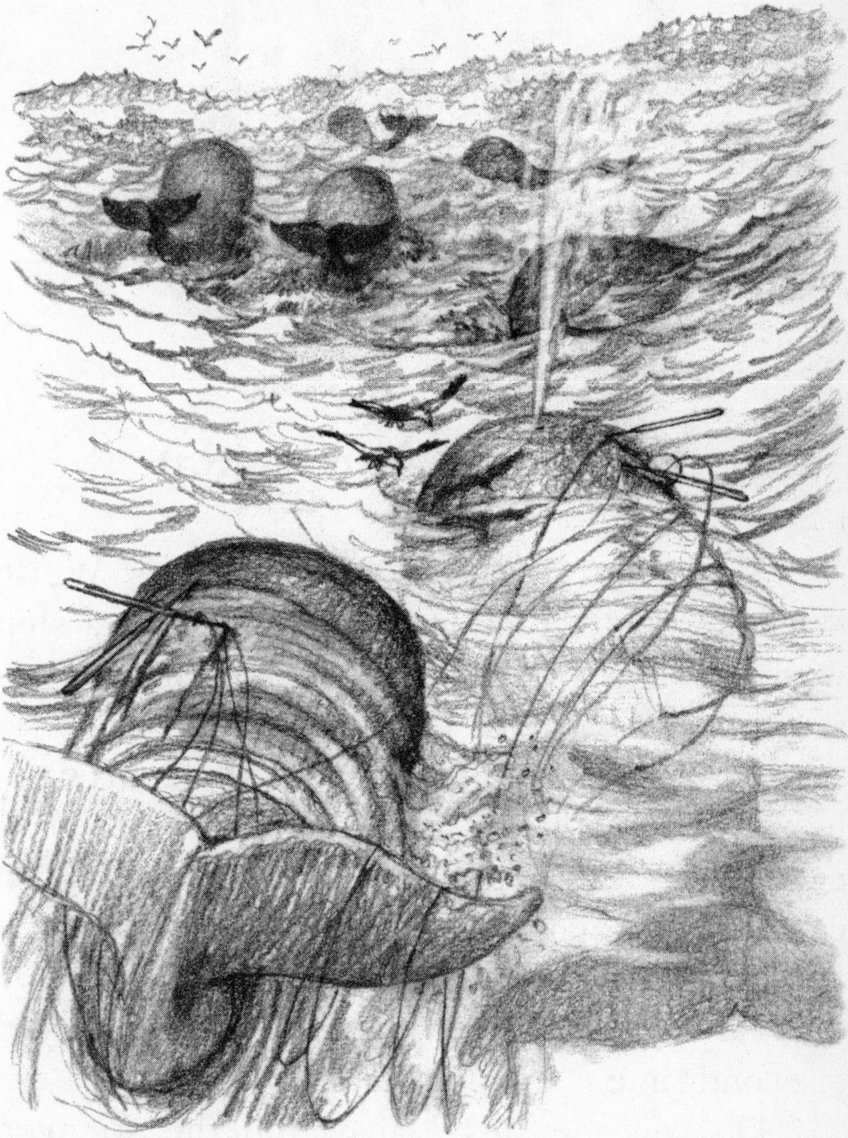

CHAPTER NINETEEN

A Warning Not Taken

"Ship, ahoy! Have ye seen the White Whale?" Ahab's familiar cry rang out, as a ship with an English flag sailed toward our ship. It was the *Samuel Enderby* of London.

The old man stood at the ship's side, his ivory leg in plain sight. As the ships drew nearer to each other, we saw that one arm of the English captain's jacket was empty and hung loosely at his side.

"Have ye seen the White Whale?" Ahab cried a second time.

"Do you see this?" answered the stranger, pulling an arm of white Sperm whale bone from under his jacket and waving it above his head.

"Man my boat!" screamed Ahab. "Prepare to lower!"

In less than a minute he was in his boat sitting below the English ship. "Tell me, man. Tell me quick! Where did ye see the White Whale?"

"There I saw him! There on the Equator last year," said the captain, his dead, white arm pointing toward the East.

"And he took your arm from you, did he?" asked Ahab.

"He did. And did he take your leg?"

"Tell me the story. Tell me the story!" Ahab shouted, becoming more excited.

The Englishman said that he had been hunting in the area of the Equator for the first time and, until then, had never heard of Moby Dick. One day, after he had found a small herd of whales and gotten a harpoon into one of them, a giant white whale rose from the deep and began snapping at the line as if he were trying to free the other whale.

"And his hump. Was it huge and wrinkled, and did it have a harpoon stuck in it?" asked Ahab.

"That it did," the captain went on. "And

when I put my own harpoon in him, he dragged me from my boat. The line hooked around my arm and tore it from my shoulder."

"That's him! That's Moby Dick!" shouted Ahab. "I put that first harpoon in him just before he took my leg. Have ye seen him since?"

"Twice more I've seen him, but I didn't chase him. I don't need to give up my other arm. I know when I've met my match. There are other whales in the sea."

"Which way did he go? Where will I find him?" Ahab cried.

"You better leave him alone," warned the Englishman, waving his whale-bone arm.

"I cannot leave him alone. I must hunt him," said Ahab. "He draws me to him. Tell me, man, what direction did he go?"

"Good heavens! What's the matter with you?" said the other captain. "He was heading east, I think." Then he turned, whispering to Fedallah, "Is your captain crazy?"

Putting his finger to his lips as if to silence the Englishman, Fedallah hurried Ahab back into his boat. Ahab's phantom, eerie crew wasted no time rowing Ahab back toward the *Pequod*.

The Englishman shouted for Ahab to listen to him, but Ahab stared straight ahead through cold, dark eyes that shone like black marbles. The wild look on Ahab's face as he struggled back up to the *Pequod*'s deck sent cold chills through me. I had a feeling that things were going to get worse, but I had no idea how *much* worse.

CHAPTER TWENTY

A New White Leg

As soon as he set foot and stump on deck, Ahab began the most furious pacing back and forth. Then, as if he wanted to look everywhere at the same time, he stuck his ivory leg in the hole in the deck and began spinning around and around in circles like a top. Suddenly, there was a sharp, screeching snap as the ivory leg broke in two. With a hateful look, Ahab ordered the carpenter and blacksmith to make him another leg.

The men worked straight through the night until a new leg was finished and fastened to Ahab's knee. Without a word of thanks, Ahab whirled and rushed back to the deck where he stood for the whole day and night. His eyes never left the seas in front of him.

There would not be much rest from now on. We were getting closer to Moby Dick.

The next day we had another kind of problem.

CHAPTER TWENTY-ONE

Queequeg's Coffin

Once a whale ship has begun to fill its barrels with oil, the men pour water over the barrels every few days to keep them damp. The dampness tightens the wood and keeps the valuable treasure from leaking out. After the barrels have been soaked, the water is pumped out and the seamen look closely at this water. If there is any sign of whale oil in the water, it means there is a leak. As you can imagine, after risking their lives to collect the oil, this causes great concern among the crew.

The pumping had been done according to schedule, and a leak was found. The bad news was passed to Starbuck, and he went to Ahab's cabin to report the serious problem. Starbuck found Ahab bent over his desk making marks on maps where Moby Dick had been seen.

"The oil is leaking down in the hold of the ship, sir. We must drop sails, pull up the barrels, and repair the leak."

"What's that ye say?" shouted Ahab. "Curse ye, man. We'll not stop for a second, not when we're nearing Moby Dick. Stop to fix some stupid barrels? Full ahead, I say!" cried Ahab, pointing to the charts in front of him.

"If we don't fix the leak, sir, we'll lose in one day all the precious oil we've come twenty thousand miles to get."

"Let it leak! I am in control of this ship, and I say let the blasted oil leak!"

Starbuck's face reddened. He begged Ahab to listen to him. This threw Ahab into a rage. He grabbed a gun from the wall, and pointed it at Starbuck.

Starbuck slowly straightened and looked into Ahab's eyes. "Thou hast angered me, sir. But thou hast no reason to fear me. I will tell thee whom thou must fear, Captain Ahab. Let Ahab beware

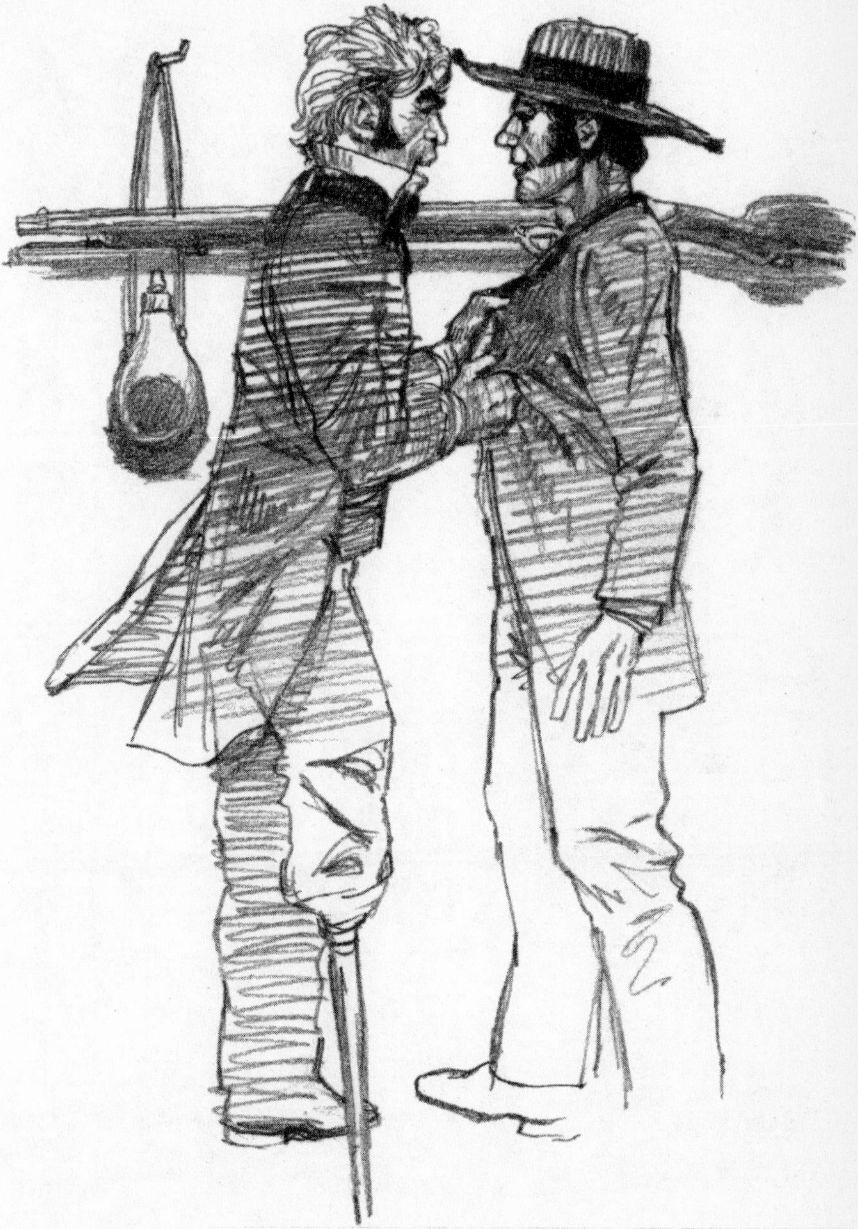

of Ahab! Beware of thyself, old man."

Starbuck turned and left, leaving Ahab alone. Soon after, his order to drop all sails and repair the barrels rang out across the decks.

The crew sprang into action and began the difficult, messy work of digging through the slimy, cold waters in the very bottom of the ship. Each barrel was moved until the leaks were found and fixed. Queequeg worked harder than I've ever seen a man work, slithering around the barrels like a spotted lizard at the bottom of a well. Sadly, with all the sweating down in that dampness, Queequeg became chilled and for a few days became so sick that I was afraid he might die.

We put Queequeg into bed and wrapped him up to keep him warm. There he lay, poor fellow, his color becoming gray and his eyes becoming more hollow as the days wore on. Not one man in the crew gave up on him, though. Then, all at once, Queequeg's eyelids fluttered, and his faint voice made a strange request.

Taking the hand of the sailor nearest to him, Queequeg whispered that he remembered the whalers of Nantucket always being laid in little wooden canoes when they died. Since this was also what the people of his native island did, Queequeg wondered if we could build a small canoe that would be his coffin. I can tell you, there was nothing we would not do for this brave man. The carpenter soon had built a canoe of the finest wood he could find.

When the canoe was brought to him, Queequeg asked that we put him in it and that his harpoon be placed at his side. Then he asked us to bring him his little wooden god, Yojo, and his boat paddle. When all of this had been done, Queequeg closed his eyes and spoke not a word for a long time.

When his eyes finally opened, there was a new shine in them, and the happy crew knew that he was getting well. A few days later, when Queequeg's strength had returned, he found a board in the carpenter's shop and began making a cover for the canoe-coffin. He spent hours carving native figures and designs on the cover, which looked like the tattoos on his body. Queequeg then said that he was ready to go back to hunting whales. He stored his harpoon and clothing in the coffin and joined the rest of the crew on deck.

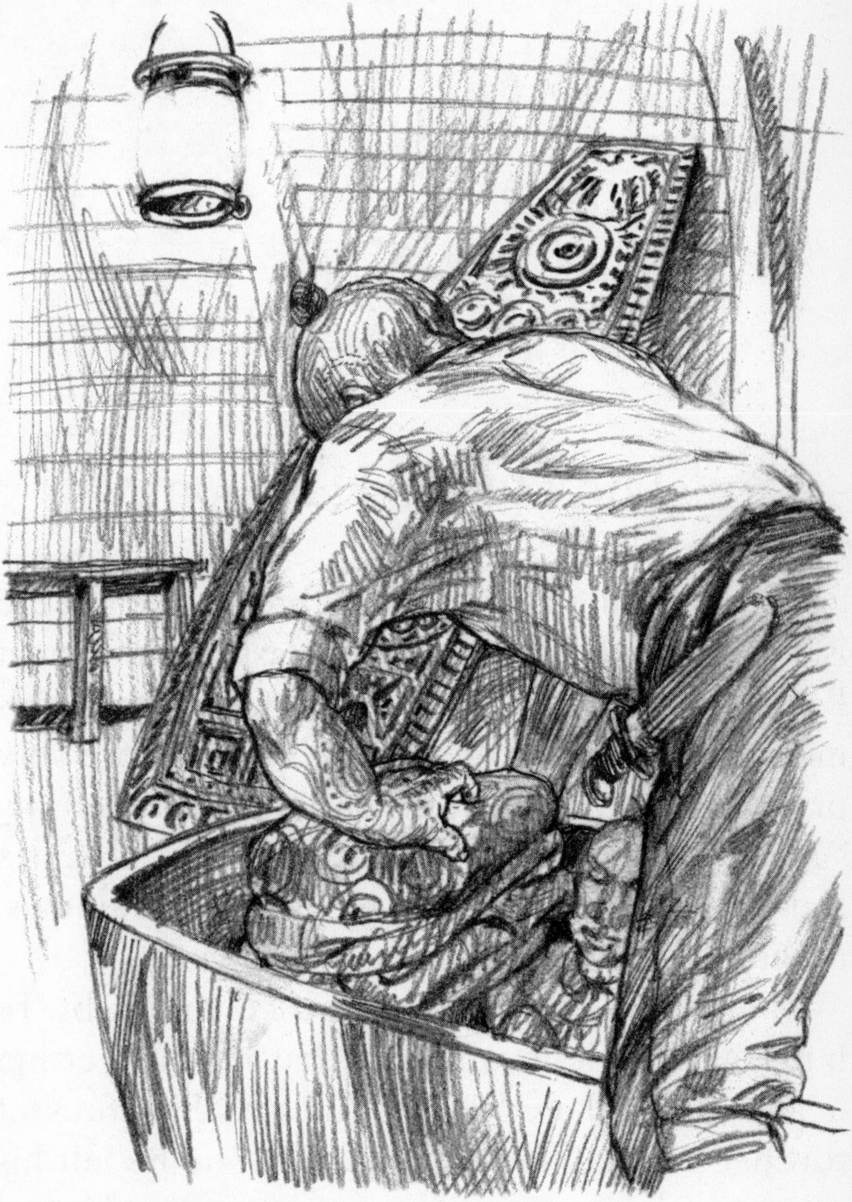

CHAPTER TWENTY-TWO

The Devil's Harpoon

Our sails filled by a friendly breeze, we left the islands behind us and glided at last into the great Pacific. Oh, how I had dreamed of these seas, this most watery part of the world. This was the very place I had pictured in my mind as I packed my suitcase many months and thousands of miles ago—the Pacific, the sea of peace. But sometimes, peaceful dreams can become nightmares.

The Pacific brought no peace to Ahab. To him, the Pacific meant only that he was getting nearer to the hated White Whale. The fires of revenge burned hotter in his soul, and he left his watch on deck only to sleep. But we even heard him cry out in his sleep, "She blows! The White Whale blows! She spouts thick blood!" The madness in the things he did grew worse.

One morning, Ahab ordered that the blacksmith build a harpoon of the hardest steel. When its point had been made sharp, he called Queequeg, Tashtego and Daggoo to his cabin. Taking blood from each of their arms, he dipped the tip of the harpoon into it and baptized the harpoon in the name of the devil. "This will be the harpoon that kills Moby Dick," he shrieked. As the days went on, the harpoon never left his hand as he thumped and tapped back and forth on his dead, white leg.

When Queequeg told me what had happened during that evil baptism, my dreams of peace ended—my nightmare had begun.

CHAPTER TWENTY-THREE

The Happy *Bachelor*

As we sailed farther into the heart of the Japanese whaling grounds, we began to see whales all around us. Often, in mild, pleasant weather, we spent ten or twenty hours each day pulling oars as we chased after them, but we had no luck. On one of these calm days, a ship came into sight. She was a ship from Nantucket named the *Bachelor*.

As the ship came closer, we saw she was on her way home, every barrel full of rich oil. Colorful flags flew from her masts, and the crews were dancing and singing. Every member of the crew wore a smile on his face. The happy captain stood up. Ahab also stood on his deck, shaggy, dark, and full of gloom.

"Come aboard, come aboard!" cried the laughing captain of the merry ship.

"Have ye seen the White Whale?" Ahab replied, scowling.

"No, only heard of him. But I don't believe in him at all. Come aboard!"

"Ye are too jolly! Sail on," muttered Ahab.

"Nonsense! Come aboard and join our party. We'll take that black look from your face," answered the captain of the *Bachelor*.

"I have no interest in your happy party," said Ahab. "Ye are a full ship. We are an empty ship. So, go your way, and I will go mine."

The two ships passed. The laughter of the *Bachelor* died away in the distance. Ahab stared at the ship until it was gone. Then he reached into his pocket and pulled out a small bottle. In the bottle were a few grains of sand from America. After looking for several minutes at the small reminder of home, he spun around on his ivory leg and ordered the crew to sail at full speed on a course that would lead him to Moby Dick.

CHAPTER TWENTY-FOUR

Fedallah's Dark Riddle

We were not a happy crew after our meeting with the *Bachelor*. The joy and laughter of the men heading for home showed us how dark and unhappy things were on the *Pequod*. We needed something to cheer us up. The following day brought a little good luck that took our minds off our problems, at least for a while.

Just before noon, whales were found and four were killed—one by Ahab. It was late in the afternoon when the chase ended, and by the time we had three of the four whales tied to the ship, the sun was setting. The crews were in a good mood.

The whale Ahab's crew had killed had not yet been brought to the ship. As darkness came, Ahab ordered his crew to stay in the boat next to their whale. There Ahab sat, bobbing up and down on the waves, staring at the whale. He could not get his hatred and bitterness toward Moby Dick out of his mind. With these dark thoughts circling in his mind, Ahab fell asleep.

Fedallah was now the only one awake in Ahab's boat. He sat quietly, mysteriously, watching the sharks twist and turn around the dead whale. One of them flapped against the side of the boat. Ahab woke up and saw Fedallah's shadowy face.

"I have had a dream, Fedallah," Ahab said. "I have dreamed of a hearse coming to carry my body away."

"Didn't I tell you of that dark mystery, old man?" said Fedallah. "You will have neither a hearse nor a coffin. But you will see two hearses on the sea before you die. The first will be one not made by human hands. The second hearse will be made only of wood grown in America."

Ahab laughed and refused to believe Fedallah.

"Believe it or not, old man. You cannot die

until these things happen. And hear these words. I shall go before you to lead the way. Even after I have gone ahead of you to death, you will see me again."

"What? Ye shall pilot me and lead me to my death?" said Ahab. "Well, let me tell ye something. Your foolish predictions only make me believe that I *shall* kill Moby Dick and still live."

"Listen closely, Ahab," warned Fedallah. "A rope will kill you."

"Never!" said Ahab. "Your warnings are so impossible to believe that I don't think I shall ever die." Ahab laughed and turned away.

Nothing more was said. The gray dawn came on, and the sleeping crew awoke. Before noon, the dead whale was brought to the ship.

CHAPTER TWENTY-FIVE

The Candles

In a few days time, we turned toward the Equator where Moby Dick had been seen. Several of the men began looking at the gold doubloon nailed to the mast, wondering who would get the prize. The ship was full of excitement. The excitement turned to terror that evening when we ran into a typhoon, the worst kind of storm there is.

The storm raged and grew worse as the night grew darker. Our sails were ripped from their masts. Sky and sea roared. The night skies were split with thunder and blazed with the lightning. Starbuck stood hanging to a line and wondered if it could get any worse. It did. Everything was out of our control. In the middle of all this fury, we saw Ahab making his way toward the ship's bare mast and pointing to the sky with his cursed harpoon.

Looking up, we saw the tops of the three masts suddenly throw off sparks and burst into flame. They looked like three gigantic candles burning before an altar. It was as if God's burning finger had been laid upon the ship.

"Have mercy on us all!" cried Stubb.

"Aye, aye, men!" shouted Ahab. "Look up at it. It is a sign. The white flame lights the way to the White Whale! The lightning is a light that leaps out of darkness, but I am a darkness that leaps out of light!"

When he spoke those words, Ahab's harpoon burst into fire and burned like a snake's tongue. Starbuck grabbed Ahab's arm. "God is against thee, old man. Beware! It is a bad journey. Let me turn the ship around and head home while we can."

The crew became restless and moved to follow Starbuck's advice. Ahab snatched the burning harpoon and held it up to the crew, swearing that he would use it on them if they

moved a muscle to turn the ship around.

"I have sworn to kill the White Whale, and ye are sworn to follow me! There is no turning back." Holding the harpoon to his lips, he blew out the flame and screamed, "I blow out the last fear!"

The sailors turned from him in terror. Only Starbuck stayed to try to talk to Ahab. But it was no use. Ahab ordered him to hold course and sail through the typhoon against the powerful forces of nature.

CHAPTER TWENTY-SIX

The Life Buoy

Steering south-eastward now, we moved even closer to the Equator and found ourselves in calm waters. The calm was suddenly broken by cries from the water. The sailor keeping the first watch of the morning had fallen from his post and was struggling for dear life to keep his head above water. An empty barrel was thrown as a life buoy, but it had become cracked and sank to the bottom along with the poor young sailor.

Queequeg suggested that since we now had no life preserver for future emergencies, we should make one from his own canoe-coffin. Starbuck ordered the coffin brought up from below, and the carpenter nailed the cover shut and sealed the cracks with tar so it would float. When they were finished, we hung it on the back of our ship.

Ahab laughed and made fun of the idea of using a box made for death as something that might save a life. Queequeg, bless him, seemed to know what he was doing. I found out later just how wise an idea this was. You shall find out, too.

CHAPTER TWENTY-SEVEN

Sad *Rachel*

The next day, still sad about the loss of our young sailor, we met the *Rachel*, a ship full of a sadness of much the same kind.

As the ship pulled near, we could see that her crew seemed full of gloom. Her captain stood to speak, but before he could get a word out, Ahab's voice rang out.

"Have ye seen the White Whale?"

"Aye, yesterday. Have you seen a lost whaleboat anywhere?"

Ahab could hardly control his joy when he heard that Moby Dick might be near. But before he could speak, the other captain had lowered a boat and climbed aboard our ship. He now faced Ahab, his eyes full of pain and worry. Ahab saw that he was a man from Nantucket whom he knew, but made no effort to greet him.

It seemed that the afternoon before, the *Rachel* had sighted Moby Dick's white hump and sent four boats after him. One boat had gotten a harpoon in him, but the whale had dived below and never came back up. The captain had called in his boats when it became dark. Only three had come back. The fourth, along with its crew, was missing. The *Rachel* had searched all night with no luck.

Having told his sad story, the captain asked Ahab to join with him in the search for his crew. Ahab gave him a cold look and made no offer to help.

"My boy—my own son—is among that crew! For God's sake, I beg you! Just help me for forty-eight hours. I'll gladly pay you. He's but a little lad, only twelve years old." The captain's eyes filled with tears.

Still, Ahab stood like a stone, his eyes cold and empty.

"I know you have a son of your own, Captain

Ahab. Think of him, safe and warm back home. Do for me what you would have me do for you." Then the captain added, "I will not go until you've agreed to help me."

"Away with ye!" cried Ahab. "Captain Gardiner, I will not do it. Even now, I am losing time. Good-bye. Good-bye. God bless ye, man, and may I forgive myself, but I must go. Starbuck, in three minutes get all the strangers off the ship and make her ready to sail!" Ahab turned and went into his cabin.

Gardiner, without a word, hurried down the side of the ship and back to his own. My heart ached as I watched his ship sail back and forth, stopping to search every dark spot in the sea.

She was like Rachel in the Bible, weeping for her children because they were not yet found.

CHAPTER TWENTY-EIGHT

We Meet the *Delight*

A ship with the name *Delight* had been sighted. I hoped that this was a good sign, for we all needed something to delight us right now. My hopes soon were destroyed by the news the ship brought. As the *Delight* came nearer, we saw a smashed whaleboat hanging from her side.

"Have ye seen the White Whale?" shouted Ahab.

"Look!" said the hollow-cheeked captain, pointing to the wrecked boat.

"Have ye killed him?" Ahab asked.

"The harpoon has not been made that will ever do that. I am burying the first of five men he killed."

"Not made?" cried Ahab, holding his harpoon

above his head. "I hold in my hand his death, baptized in blood and hardened by lightning bolts."

"Then God be with you, old man." The captain turned to his crew and ordered that they prepare to release the body of the dead sailor to its ocean grave. He began to pray.

"Sail on! Sail on!" screamed Ahab. But we had not sailed quickly enough to avoid hearing the splash of the body as it fell into the sea.

We turned away from the *Delight*. Her captain saw the coffin hanging on the rear of our ship. "Ha! Look men!" he cried. "She turns her back on our sad burial and shows us her own coffin!"

As we headed east under full sail, my fears returned. The *Delight* had brought no delight.

CHAPTER TWENTY-NINE

The Chase—First Day

From that moment on, Ahab would not leave the deck. With weird Fedallah at his side, he paced, and turned, and whirled from one end of the ship to the other. What little he ate, he ate standing up.

One night, Ahab stopped short in the middle of his pacing. He raised his face to the sky and began sniffing the air like a hunting dog. He said he could smell a whale and ordered the men to drop the sails and stay in that spot for the night. His nose proved right, for at daybreak a faint rippling path in the sea told us that something below was stirring the surface.

"Man the mastheads! Call all hands! Tell me what ye see!"

When the crew reported they saw nothing, Ahab ordered that he be lifted to the top of the mast. When he was nearly at the top, he let out a wild shriek. "There she blows! There she blows! A hump like a huge hill of snow! It is Moby Dick!"

The crew rushed to the ship's side to get a look at the thing they had been chasing for over two years. There, about a mile ahead, the whale rolled his hump and sent his spout into the air. The silent, silvery jet reminded the crew of the mysterious spirit spout they had seen in the moonlight of other oceans.

"And did none of ye see it?" asked Ahab. "Was I the first? Yes, it was I. The gold doubloon is mine. None of ye could have found the White Whale. Only I! There he is again! Again! He dives! Drop sails! Stand by to lower three boats. Starbuck, ye stay here and take care of the ship. Lower me from the mast! Faster! Now boats! To the boats!"

Soon all the boats but Starbuck's were dropped. Ahab's took the lead boat. The oars pulled through the water as all three crews began

to make their way out. Fedallah stood in Ahab's boat; a pale death-glimmer lit up his sunken eyes. Like silent fish, the boats sailed through the sea toward the White Whale.

The ocean became calm and smooth as if a carpet had been thrown over its waves. Ahab could see the huge wrinkled hump now as it rose in front of him. Hundreds of white sea birds circled above his boat. Now and then one swooped down to land on a harpoon that stuck straight up from the white back of the whale. Moby Dick moved on quietly, still hiding his lower body below the surface.

Suddenly, the calm was broken and the water exploded as the beast arched its body into the air, its cruel jaws wide open. Just as suddenly it dove, throwing its monstrous tail twenty feet above the sea before it went out of sight. The white birds still circled above the pool where the whale had last been seen.

With their oars in the air, the three boats floated quietly and waited for Moby Dick. Ahab stared into the water—looking, watching, waiting. Ahab's eyes were on a white spot rising upward from below and growing larger every

second that it rose. In the next instant, Moby
Dick's huge jaw with its two rows of crooked
teeth burst through the surface. Ahab grabbed
his special harpoon and rushed to the front of his
boat. As if he knew Ahab's plan, the whale rolled

on its side, opened its jaws, fastened them around Ahab's boat, and began shaking it like a cat playing with a mouse. Furious with the creature he hated and seeing it so near to him, Ahab grabbed the jawbone with his bare hands and wildly tried to pull it free of its grip on his boat. The bone slipped from his hands. But then the huge jaws closed just six inches from Ahab's head like a pair of huge scissors. Ahab's boat snapped in two like a toothpick. Ahab was tossed into the sea like a rag doll.

Moby Dick backed away and watched from a distance for a moment. The crew floated helplessly in the two halves of the boat. All at once, the whale began swimming in circles round and round the boat. Moby Dick swam faster and faster, as if the sight of the splintered boat angered him. Ahab's head popped in and out of the bubbling foam. He shouted for Starbuck to steer the ship at the whale. As the *Pequod* came at him, Moby Dick swam away. The boats rushed to pick up their captain. Ahab tumbled into Stubb's boat. His eyes were bloodshot, and his hair was twisted and caked with salt.

"The harpoon," he gasped. "Is it safe?"

"Aye, sir, for it was never thrown. It is here with me," answered Stubb.

When Ahab was back on board the ship, Starbuck tried again to talk him into giving up the madness. But the demons within Ahab would not let him go.

A light fog crept over the water. A few hundred yards from the ship, a mountainous forehead broke the water's surface and waited. The first day had been a good one for Moby Dick.

CHAPTER THIRTY

The Chase—Second Day

Our ship had stayed on the same course all night. Ahab knew that whales usually continued in the same direction. So, when he came on deck the next morning, he was sure Moby Dick could not be far away.

"Have ye seen him?" shouted Ahab to the lookouts on the masts.

"Nothing yet, sir. Not a thing," came the reply.

"All men on deck! Faster ahead at full sail on our same course! He swims faster than I thought, but he'll not escape. I've come around the world to kill him, and kill him I will." Ahab barked out his orders in rapid bursts.

"There she blows! There blows a spout straight ahead!" came a cry from the mast.

"Aye, ha, ha!" said Stubb. "I knew it. I knew you'd not escape, whale. A madman is after you. Ahab will drain you of your blood!"

Thirty men sprang into action, and all eyes searched the sea. For a long time they saw nothing. Suddenly, shouts rang out as Moby Dick's whole body burst forth not a mile in front of the ship.

"There she leaps! She breaches!" was the cry, as the whale came completely out of the water before crashing back to the surface.

"Yes! Lift yourself one last time to the sun, Moby Dick!" cried Ahab. "Your harpoon and your hour of death are near! Stand by all boats!"

Three boats were lowered to the water. As he had the previous day, Ahab told Starbuck to stay on the ship and keep close to the boats. Ahab and his crew leaped into one of the three boats, Fedallah standing at the front.

As if he had decided on a quick strike of his own, Moby Dick had turned and now was headed directly at the boats. Ahab shouted for the crews to stay where they were and meet the whale head-on.

The whale's furious speed and lashing tail tossed the boats like toy ships in a child's bathtub. Harpoons were thrown and stuck in his back. Moby Dick only swam faster and made charge after charge. The lines attached to the harpoons became tangled and wrapped around all three boats. Ahab cut the lines from his harpoon, but Moby Dick dragged the other two boats behind him, and with one flip of his tail threw the boats into the air and the men into the sea.

Stubb and Flask screamed out for help as they fought to stay afloat. Sharks began to circle. Ahab, free of the lines, turned his boat toward them. At that instant, Moby Dick came up from the depths at full speed and crashed his head into the bottom of Ahab's boat. The boat rose straight up in the air as if it had been shot from a cannon. It tumbled over and over and fell back to the sea, its crew trapped beneath. Ahab made his way out from under the crushed boat and clung to its splintered side. As if satisfied, Moby Dick backed away and watched quietly for a moment. Then he turned his broad tail and swam slowly away.

When the fury of the battle had ended, Starbuck brought the ship into position to rescue

the men. One by one, the men and pieces of the boats were pulled from the water. As Ahab was brought up we saw that his ivory leg had been snapped off, leaving but a short, sharp splinter. He leaned on Starbuck's shoulder and ordered that the spare boats be made ready. The carpenter promised to make him a new leg.

After asking about Moby Dick and the direction he had headed, Ahab ordered a roll call of the crew to see if any were missing. There was no sign of Fedallah. Starbuck told Ahab he had seen the lines of the harpoon wrap around Fedallah. He was sure that Moby Dick had dragged Fedallah under. Ahab whispered something under his breath:

"Fedallah—Fedallah!—gone, gone? *And he told me he would die before me!* Yet he also said *I would see him again before I die.* What's that to mean? It's a tough riddle, but I'll solve it."

As with the evening before, we dropped sail and got ready for a third battle. The sounds of hammers, saws, and grindstones were heard all night as the crews prepared spare boats and sharpened new harpoons. Meanwhile, the carpenter built a new leg for Ahab out of a piece of Ahab's own wrecked boat. Those who had not been injured stayed busy making bandages for the others' wounds.

Ahab swore that tomorrow would be the last day of Moby Dick's life. He remained on deck a long while, staring into the distance. His eyes never left the sea as shadows cast by the full moon flickered back and forth across the ugly scar on his face. In the distance, another scarred head waited, as before.

CHAPTER THIRTY-ONE

The Chase—Third Day

The morning of the third day dawned fair and fresh. The sea was quiet and calm—almost too calm. Just as soon as the sun had risen, every mast was dotted with men on daylight watch.

"D'ye see him?" cried Ahab. But the whale was nowhere in sight.

"Just keep following that path of ripples his great tail leaves for us. Hold a straight course. What a lovely day again! It seems a new world— a summer house to the angels. A nicer day could not dawn upon this world. The warm winds blow my good ship on, and something as steady as the wind blows my soul along. On with it! Aloft there, in the masts! What d'ye see?"

"Nothing, sir."

"Nothing! Do none of ye see the White Whale? And it's nearly noon! Yes, the sun, I see it now. It must be that we sailed past him in the night. Aye, he's chasing *me* now, and I am not chasing *him*. That's bad. Turn around! Sail back the way we came!"

Returning in the opposite direction, the *Pequod* sailed directly against the wind, plowing through the foam of its own path.

"Now he steers against the wind for the open jaw," murmured Starbuck. "God keep us, but already my bones feel damp and my flesh wet from the inside. I fear that I disobey my God by obeying him!"

"Swing me up to the mast!" screamed Ahab. "We should meet him soon."

A whole hour passed. Even the air around us seemed to hold its breath. But at last, Ahab spied the spout again.

"Forehead to forehead I meet thee this third time, Moby Dick! He's too far off to lower boats yet, Mr. Starbuck. He travels fast and I must get down from here. But let me have one last look at

the sea from here—an old sight, but somehow still so young. It hasn't changed a bit since I first saw it as a boy from the sand hills of Nantucket. It's the same—the same to Noah as to me.

"But good-bye, farewell, old ship. We both grow old together. And what about Fedallah? He said I would see him again before I die. But where? Will I have eyes at the bottom of the sea if I should happen to go down those dark stairs? Good-bye, masthead. Keep a good eye upon the whale while I'm gone. We'll talk tomorrow—no, tonight, when Moby Dick is dead."

Ahab gave the word and was steadily lowered through the blue air to the deck. Shortly, the boats were lowered. Ahab waved from his boat to Starbuck on deck.

"Starbuck!"

"Sir?"

"For the third time my soul sets out on this hunt, Starbuck."

"Aye, sir. That is what you want."

"Some ships sail from home and are never seen again, Starbuck."

"It's true, sir—sad, but true."

"Starbuck, I am old. Shake hands with me,

man." Ahab held his hand up from his boat.

Their hands met. Starbuck had tears in his eyes.

"Oh, my captain, my captain!—don't go—don't go! I am a brave man, but I cry when I think of what thou art about to do."

"Lower me away!" cried Ahab, tossing Starbuck's arm from him. "Stand by the crew! Man the boats!"

Not even the good sense of loyal Starbuck could change Ahab's mind. Sharks surrounded Ahab's boat, snapping and tearing at its oars. Starbuck shuddered as he watched Ahab's boat pull away. He thought about his wife and little boy, and his home he might never see again. As he looked upward to the heavens, a hawk tore the red flag from the ship's mast and flew away.

The boats had not gone far when Ahab realized that Moby Dick lay somewhere deep below. He stopped and held his boat against the waves directly over the spot where the whale had disappeared when it dove. "Ha! Strike, you waves. But you strike a thing with no cover! There can be no coffin without a lid. There will be no hearse for me. And only a rope can kill me! Ha! Ha!"

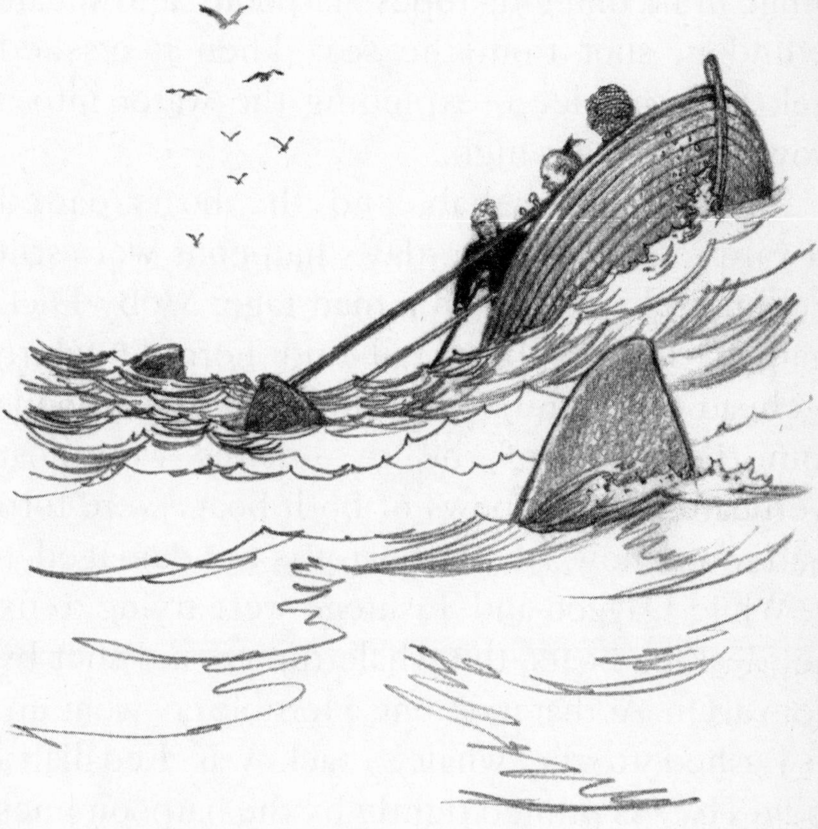

Suddenly the waters around him swelled in wide circles, then rose up as if an iceberg were pushing from below. There was a low, rumbling sound—a deep hum. Everyone held his breath as a huge hulk, dragging ropes, harpoons, and spears behind it, shot from the sea. Then it crashed back into the deep, exploding the water into a shower thirty feet high.

"Now!" cried Ahab, and the boats darted forward to attack. Yesterday's harpoons were still sticking in him. As if in a mad rage, Moby Dick charged. His flapping tail and horrible white forehead threw the boats aside. All the harpoons from the boats of the two mates were lost overboard and the bows of both boats were torn apart. Somehow, Ahab's boat was not damaged.

While Daggoo and Tashtego were trying to fix their leaking boats, the whale turned and shot by them again. At that moment, a terrible cry went up.

Lashed to the whale's back was Fedallah's body! He was pinned tightly by the harpoon lines which the monster's rolling had wrapped around him. His braided hair was in wild shreds, and his bulging eyes were staring straight at old Ahab.

The harpoon dropped from Ahab's hand.

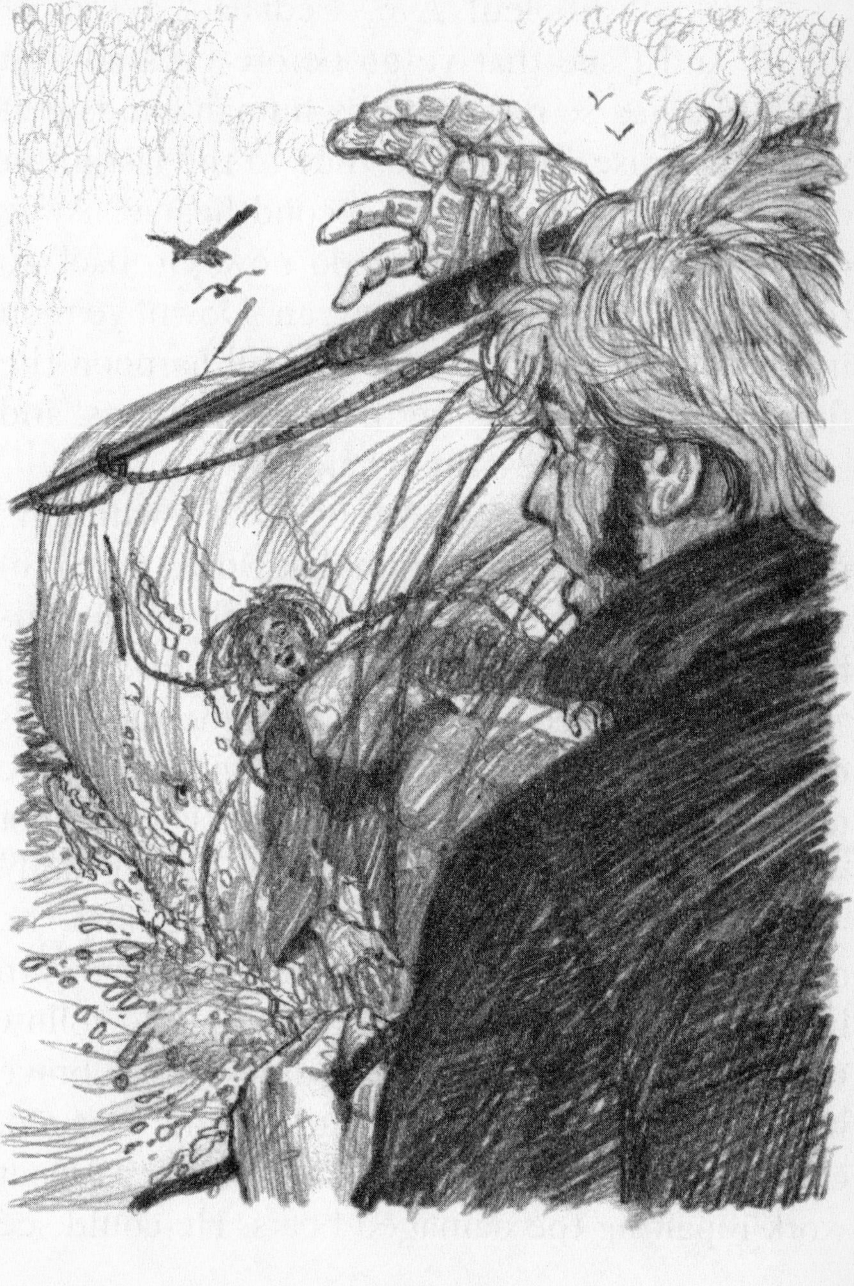

"Tricked! Fooled! Aye, Fedallah, I see ye again! And I see that ye go before me and that this is the hearse not made by human hands that ye did promise. But I hold thee to the last letter of thy word. Where is the second hearse? Away mates! Your boats are no good now. Go back to the ship and repair them if ye can. Down, ye men in my boat! If ye dare to leave, I'll harpoon the first man to jump! Ye are my arms and legs, and so obey me. Where's the whale?"

He turned and saw Moby Dick swimming past the *Pequod* in a direction that would take him away from them and out to sea. Ahab headed his boat toward the whale.

"Oh, Ahab!" cried Starbuck from the ship. "It is not too late, even now on the third day, not too late to stop the mad chase. See! Moby Dick is not seeking ye. It is ye, ye, who are madly seeking him!"

As Ahab's boat passed nearby the ship, he could see Starbuck's face at the rail. Waving to him, Ahab told him to turn the ship and follow the whale. Looking up he could see the brave harpooners, Queequeg, Tashtego, and Daggoo, climbing the three masts. Carpenters were at work repairing the damaged boats. He could see

Stubb and Flask, busy making new harpoons. As he heard the hammers working on the broken boats, another hammer seemed to drive a nail into his heart. He saw that the flag was gone from the mast and he shouted to Tashtego to be sure to get another flag and nail it to the top.

Ahab looked back toward the water and saw Moby Dick charging straight at him. When he passed close enough, Ahab stood and flung his fierce harpoon and cursed the hated whale.

With the sting of the steel, Moby Dick tossed the boat into the air with his tail. Three men were thrown into the sea. Two were able to swim to the boat's side and struggle back in. The third man drifted away in the sea, swimming and calling for help. His voice could not be heard above the roar of the waves.

Moby Dick now turned himself and his anger at our ship. Picking up speed as he went, he pointed his powerful white head at the *Pequod*. The crew all saw him coming at the same time. Tashtego, who was nailing the new flag to the mast, stopped his arm in mid-air. Stubb and Flask dropped their half-built harpoons. Starbuck stared at the approaching creature and

began to pray. Queequeg, Daggoo, and the rest of the crew did not move. Their eyes were locked on the giant beast rushing toward the ship. With a sickening crunch, a hundred tons of muscle, bone and white anger crashed into the ship. Men and masts shook and fell as the sea waters rushed like a river through the hole in the ship's side.

"The ship! The hearse! The second hearse!" cried Ahab from the boat. "Its wood could only be American!"

Ahab turned from the sinking, dying ship to see Moby Dick lying still in the water. Coming nearer to the whale, Ahab picked up the last harpoon and shouted out a string of oaths and curses full of hate.

"For evil's sake I stab at thee! For hate's sake I spit my last breath at thee. Let all coffins and hearses sink into the same pool! Now I give you my final spear!"

The harpoon struck. The injured whale flew forward, pulling the harpoon line with it at lightning speed. The line looped and twisted. Ahab bent to clear the line, and when he did, it caught and tightened like a noose around his neck. Without a sound, Ahab shot out of the boat.

Before the crew even knew he was gone, he had disappeared into the ocean—killed by his own rope. Fedallah's dark promise had come true.

For an instant, the poor crew in Ahab's boat looked in shock, then turned. "The ship! Great God, where is the ship?" Their eyes filled with terror when they saw only the top parts of the masts still above water. There on the masts hung the harpooners, still keeping their lookouts on the sea. Now, a great whirlpool formed as the ship slipped further down into the water. The force of the whirlpool's pull caught the small boat. With one last rushing sound, the crew, every oar, every harpoon, and every last splinter of the *Pequod* were drawn to the center of the black hole and carried out of sight.

Small birds flew crying over the whirlpool. Slowly, the sides of the dark watery hole slid to its center and the water became still and calm. The great shroud of the sea rolled on as it rolled five thousand years ago.

CHAPTER THIRTY-TWO

The Rest of the Story

And I only am escaped alone to tell thee. —Job

The story is over. The action is done. Why then is someone speaking?—Because one did survive the wreck.

It so happened that after Fedallah's disappearance, I was the one picked to take his place in Ahab's boat. I was among those three seamen who, on that last day, were tossed from the rocking boat, and I was the one who floated away, given up for lost.

As I watched with horror from a distance, the whirlpool's edge began to pull me slowly to its center. By the time I neared that point, the water had begun to calm down and was just a creamy pool, turning slowly around. I floated in lazy circles around the dark hole until, all at once, up from the center shot the coffin life buoy built by my friend, Queequeg. It landed near me and floated by my side.

I was held above water by that coffin for almost one whole day and night, floating on a calm, peaceful sea. Even the circling sharks glided by as if their jaws were locked shut. The savage sea vultures sailed with closed beaks. On the second day, a sail drew near, and picked me up at last.

It was the sad *Rachel*. In her search for her missing children she found only me, Ishmael.

THE END

HERMAN MELVILLE

Herman Melville was born on August 1, 1819, in New York City, the third child in a family of eight children. When Herman was only twelve years old, his father died, leaving the family with little money.

Herman worked at a variety of jobs to help support himself and his family. He got his first taste of the sea in 1839 when he sailed on a merchant ship to Liverpool, England, and back. Two years later, he signed on the whale ship *Acushnet*, which took him throughout the Pacific over the next three years.

By 1844, Melville had seen enough of harsh sea life and settled down to write about his adventures. He was married in 1847 to Elizabeth Shaw, a childhood friend. His first sea story, *Typee*, was published two years later. He completed *Moby Dick* in 1851.

Melville authored scores of books and articles. His last novel, *Billy Budd*, was completed just months before his death on September 28, 1891. Over the years, Melville has come to be regarded as one of America's great writers, and *Moby Dick* his greatest achievement.